THE
Last
Dragonslayer

JASPER FFORDE

THE CHRONICLES OF KAZAM • BOOK ONE

THE
Last
Dragonslayer

Houghton Mifflin Harcourt
Boston   New York

For information about permission to reproduce selections from this book,
write to Permissions, Houghton Mifflin Harcourt Publishing Company,
215 Park Avenue South, New York, New York 10003.

www.hmhco.com

The text of this book is set in Garamond 3LT Std.

Library of Congress Cataloging-in-Publication Data is available.

ISBN 978-0-547-73847-5 hardcover
ISBN 978-0-544-10471-6 paperback

Manufactured in the United States of America

DOC 10 9 8 7 6 5

4500520384

For Stella Morel

1897–1933

2010–

The grandmother I never knew

The daughter I will

ONCE, I WAS FAMOUS. My face was seen on T-shirts, badges, commemorative mugs, and posters. I made front-page news, appeared on TV, and was even a special guest on *The Yogi Baird Daytime TV Show.* The *Daily Clam* called me "the year's most influential teenager," and I was the *Mollusc on Sunday*'s Woman of the Year. Two people tried to kill me, I was threatened with jail, had fifty-eight offers of marriage, and was outlawed by King Snodd IV. All that and more besides, and in less than a week.

My name is Jennifer Strange.

ONE

Practical Magic

I t looked set to become even hotter by the afternoon, just when the job was becoming more fiddly and needed extra concentration. But the fair weather brought at least one advantage: dry air makes magic work better and fly farther. Moisture has a moderating effect on the mystical arts. No sorcerer worth their sparkle ever did productive work in the rain — which probably accounts for why getting showers to *start* was once considered easy, but getting them to *stop* was nearly impossible.

We hadn't been able to afford a company car for years, so the three sorcerers, the beast, and I were packed into my rust-and-orange-but-mostly-rust Volkswagen for the short journey from Hereford to Dinmore. Lady

Mawgon had insisted on sitting in the passenger seat because "that's how it will be," which meant that Wizard Moobin and the well-proportioned Full Price were in the back seat, with the Quarkbeast sitting between the two of them and panting in the heat. I was driving, which might have been unusual anywhere but here in the Kingdom of Hereford, which was unique in the Ununited Kingdoms for having driving tests based on maturity, not age. That explained why I'd had a license since I was thirteen, while some were still failing to make the grade at forty. It was lucky I could. Sorcerers are easily distracted, and letting them drive is about as safe as waving around a chain saw at full throttle in a crowded nightclub.

We had lots to talk about—the job we were driving to, the weather, experimental spells, King Snodd's sometimes eccentric ways. But we didn't. Price, Moobin, and Mawgon, despite being our best sorcerers, didn't really get along. It wasn't anything personal; sorcerers are just like that—temperamental, and apt to break out into petulant posturing that takes time and energy to smooth over. My job of running Kazam Mystical Arts Management was less about spells and enchantments, diplomacy and bureaucracy, than about babysitting. Working with those versed in the Mystical Arts was sometimes like trying to knit with wet spaghetti: just when you thought you'd gotten somewhere, it all came to pieces in your hands. But I didn't really mind. Were they frustrating? Frequently. Were they boring? Never.

"I do wish you wouldn't do that," said Lady Mawgon in an aggrieved tone as she shot a disapproving glance at Full Price. He was changing from a human to a walrus and then back again in slow, measured transformations. The Quarkbeast was staring at him strangely, and with each transformation there wafted an unpleasant smell of fish around the small car. It was good the windows were open. To Lady Mawgon, who in better days had once been sorceress to royalty, transforming within potential view of the public was the mark of the hopelessly ill-bred.

"Groof, groof," said Full Price, trying to speak while a walrus, which is never satisfactory. "I'm just tuning up," he added in an indignant fashion, once de-walrussed or re-humaned, depending on which way you looked at it. "Don't tell me you don't need to."

Wizard Moobin and I looked at Lady Mawgon, eager to know how she *was* tuning up. Moobin had prepared for the job by tinkering with the print of the *Hereford Daily Eyestrain*. He had filled in the crossword in the twenty minutes since we'd left Kazam. Not unusual in itself, since the *Eyestrain*'s crossword is seldom hard, except that he had used printed letters from elsewhere on the page and *dragged* them across using the power of his mind alone. The crossword was now complete and more or less correct — but it left an article on Queen Mimosa's patronage of the Troll War Widows Fund looking a little disjointed.

"I am not required to answer your question," replied Lady Mawgon haughtily, "and what's more, I detest the term *tuning up.* It's *quazafucating* and always has been."

"Using the old language makes us sound archaic and out of touch," replied Price.

"It makes us sound as we are meant to be," replied Lady Mawgon, "of a noble calling."

Of a once *noble calling,* thought Moobin, inadvertently broadcasting his subconscious on an alpha so low, even I could sense it.

Lady Mawgon swiveled in her seat to glare at him. "Keep your thoughts to yourself, young man."

Moobin thought something to her but in high alpha, so only she could hear it. I don't know what he thought, but Lady Mawgon said, "Well!" and stared out the side window in an aggrieved fashion.

I sighed. This was my life.

Of the forty-five sorcerers, movers, soothsayers, shifters, weather-mongers, carpeteers, and other assorted mystical artisans at Kazam, most were fully retired due to infirmity, insanity, or damage to the vital index fingers, either through accident or rheumatoid arthritis. Of these forty-five, thirteen were potentially capable of working, but only nine had current licenses — two carpeteers, a pair of pre-cogs, and most important, five sorcerers legally empowered to carry out Acts of Enchantment. Lady Mawgon was certainly the crabbiest and probably the most skilled. As with everyone else at Kazam, her powers had faded dramatically over the past three decades or so, but unlike everyone else, she'd not really come to terms with it. In her defense, she'd had farther to fall than the rest of them, but this wasn't really an excuse. The Sisters Karamazov could also claim once-royal patronage, and they were nice as apricot pie. Mad as a knapsack of onions, but pleasant nonetheless.

I might have felt sorrier for Mawgon if she weren't so difficult all the time. Her intimidating manner made me feel small and ill at ease, and she rarely if ever missed an opportunity to put me in my place. Since Mr. Zambini's disappearance, she'd gotten worse, not better.

"Quark," said the Quarkbeast.

"Did we really have to bring the beast?" Full Price asked me.

"It jumped in the car when I opened the door."

The Quarkbeast yawned, revealing several rows of razor-sharp fangs. Despite his placid nature, the beast's ferocious appearance almost guaranteed that no one ever completely shrugged off the possibility that he might try to take a chunk out of them when they weren't looking. If the Quarkbeast was aware of this, it didn't show. Indeed, he might have been so unaware that he wondered why people always ran away screaming.

"I would be failing in my duty as acting manager of Kazam," I said, in an attempt to direct the sorcerers away from grumpiness and more in the direction of teamwork, "if I didn't mention how important this job is. Mr. Zambini always said that Kazam needed to adapt to survive, and if we get this right, we could possibly tap a lucrative market that we badly need."

"Humph!" said Lady Mawgon.

"We all need to be in *tune* and ready to hit the ground running," I added. "I told Mr. Digby we'd all be finished by six this evening."

They didn't argue. I think they knew the score well enough. In silent answer, Lady Mawgon snapped her fingers, and the Volkswagen's gearbox, which up until that moment had been making an expensive-sounding rumbling noise, suddenly fell silent. If Mawgon could replace gearbox bushings while the engine was running, she was tuned enough for all of them.

I knocked on the door of a red-brick house at the edge of the village, and a middle-aged man with a ruddy face answered.

"Mr. Digby? My name is Jennifer Strange of Kazam, acting manager for Mr. Zambini. We spoke on the phone."

He looked me up and down. "You seem a bit young to be running an agency."

"I'm sixteen," I said in a friendly manner.

"Sixteen?"

"In two weeks I'll be sixteen, yes."

"Then you're actually fifteen?"

I thought for a moment."I'm in my sixteenth *year*."

Mr. Digby narrowed his eyes."Then shouldn't you be in school or something?"

"Indentured servitude," I answered as brightly as I could, trying to sidestep the contempt that most free citizens have for people like me. As a foundling, I had been brought up by the Sisterhood, who'd sold me to Kazam four years before. I still had two years of unpaid work before I could even *think* of applying for the first level that would one day lead me, fourteen tiers of paperwork and bureaucracy later, to freedom.

"Indentured or not," replied Mr. Digby, "where's Mr. Zambini?"

"He's indisposed at present," I replied, attempting to sound as mature as I could. "I have temporarily assumed his responsibilities."

" 'Temporarily assumed his responsibilities'?" Mr.

Digby repeated. He looked at the three sorcerers, who stood waiting at the car. "Why her and not one of you?"

"Bureaucracy is for little people," retorted Lady Mawgon in an imperious tone.

"I am too busy, and paperwork exacerbates my receding hair issues," said Full Price.

"We have complete confidence in Jennifer," added Wizard Moobin, who appreciated what I did perhaps more than most. "Foundlings mature quickly. May we get started?"

"Very well," replied Mr. Digby, after a long pause in which he looked at us all in turn with a *should I cancel?* sort of look. But he didn't, and eventually went and fetched his hat and coat. "But we agreed you'd be finished by six, yes?"

I said that this was so, and he handed me his house keys. After taking a wide berth to avoid the Quarkbeast, he climbed into his car and drove away. It's not a good idea to have civilians around when sorcery is afoot. Even the stoutest incantations carry redundant strands of spell that can cause havoc if allowed to settle on the general public. Nothing serious ever happened; it was mostly rapid nose hair growth, oinking like a pig, blue pee, that sort of stuff. It soon wore off, but it was bad for business.

"Right," I said to the sorcerers. "Over to you."

They looked at each other, then at the ordinary suburban house.

"I used to conjure up storms," said Lady Mawgon with a sigh.

"So could we all," replied Wizard Moobin.

"Quark," said the Quarkbeast.

None of the sorcerers had rewired a house by spell before, but by reconfiguring the root directory on the core spell language of ARAMAIC, it could be done with relative ease—as long as the three of them pooled their resources. It had been Mr. Zambini's idea to move Kazam into the home improvement market. Charming moles out of gardens, resizing stuff for the self-storage industry, and finding lost things was easy work, but it didn't pay well. Using magic to rewire a house, however, was quite different. Unlike electricians, we didn't need to touch the house in order to do it. No mess, no problems, and all finished in under a day.

I stood by my Volkswagen to be near the car radio-phone, the most reliable form of mobile communication we had these days. Any calls to the Kazam office would ring here. I wasn't just Kazam's manager; I was also the receptionist, booking clerk, and taxi service. I had to look after the forty-five sorcerers, deal with the shabby building that housed us all, and fill out the numerous forms that the Magical Powers (amended 1966) Act required when even the *tiniest* spell was undertaken. I did all this because (1) the Great Zambini couldn't because he was missing, (2) I'd been part of Kazam since I was twelve and knew the Mystical Arts Management business inside out, and (3) no one else wanted to.

I looked across to where Wizard Moobin, Lady Mawgon, and Full Price were still sizing up the house. Sorcery wasn't about mumbling a spell and letting fly — it was more a case of appraising the problem, planning the various incantations to greatest effect, *then* letting fly. The three of them were still in the appraising stage, which generally meant a good deal of staring, tea, discussion, argument, more discussion, tea, and more staring.

The phone bleeped.

"Jenny? It's Perkins."

The Youthful Perkins was one of the only young sorcerers at Kazam and was serving a loose apprenticeship. His particular field of interest was Remote Suggestion, although he wasn't very good at it. He'd once attempted to get us to like him more by sending out a broad *Am I cool or what?!* suggestion on the wide subalpha, but he mixed it up with the suggestion that he often cheated at Scrabble, and then wondered why everyone stared at him and shook their heads sadly. It had been very amusing until it wore off, but not to Perkins. Because we were close to the same age, we got along fairly well and I kind of liked him. But since this might have been a *suggestion* generated by him, I had no way of knowing if I truly liked him or not.

"Hey, Perkins," I said. "Did you get Patrick off to work in time?"

"Just about. But I think he's back on the marzipan again."

This was worrying. Patrick of Ludlow was a Mover. Although not possessed of the sharpest mind, he was kind and gentle and exceptionally gifted at levitation. He earned a regular wage for Kazam by removing illegally parked cars for the city. It took a lot of effort — he would sleep fourteen hours of twenty-four — and the marzipan echoed back to a darker time in his life that he didn't care to speak of.

"So what's up?"

"The Sisterhood sent round your replacement. What do you want me to do with him?"

I'd been wondering when this would happen. The Sisterhood traditionally supplied Kazam with a foundling every four years, as it took a long time to train someone in the somewhat unique set of skills and mildly elastic regard for reality required for Mystical Arts Management, and the dropout rate was high. Sharon Zoiks had been the fourth, I had been the sixth, and this new one would be the seventh. We didn't talk about the fifth.

"Pop him in a taxi and send him up. No, cancel that. It'll be too expensive. Ask Nasil to carpet him up. Usual precautions. Cardboard box?"

"Absolutely. By the way, I've got two tickets to see Sir Matt Grifflon live in concert. Do you want to go?"

"Who with?"

"With? *Me,* of course."

"I'll think about it."

"Right," he said, then mumbled something about how he knew at least twelve people who would literally kill to see singing sensation Sir Matt, and hung up.

In truth, I would very much like to see Sir Matt Grifflon in concert. Aside from being one of King Snodd's favorites, he was a recording star and quite handsome in a lantern-jaw-and-flowing-mane kind of way. But I decided I should pass, despite my curiosity about finding out what going on a date was like. Even if Perkins *was* using some beguiling spell, it was a bad idea to get involved with anyone in the Mystical Arts. There is a very good reason why sorcerers are all single. Love and magic are like oil and water—they just don't mix.

I stood and watched the three sorcerers stare at the house from every direction, apparently doing nothing. I knew better than to ask them what was going on or how they were doing. A moment's distraction could unravel a spell in a twinkling. Moobin and Price were dressed casually and without any metal, for fear of burns, but Lady Mawgon was in traditional garb. She wore long black crinolines that rustled like leaves when she walked and often sparkled in the darkness. During the kingdom's frequent power cuts, I could always tell when it was she gliding down one of Zambini Towers' endless corridors. Once, in a daring moment, someone had pinned stars and a moon cut from silver foil to her black dress, which made her incandescent with rage. She ranted to Mr. Zambini for almost twenty minutes about how no one was taking their calling seriously, and how could she be expected to work with such infantile nincompoops? Zambini spoke to everyone in turn, but he probably found it as funny as the rest of us. We never discovered who did it, but I reckoned it was Full Price.

With little else to do except keep an eye on the three sorcerers, I sat down on a handy garden bench and read Wizard Moobin's newspaper. The text that he had moved around the paper was still out of place, and I frowned. Tuning spells like these were usually temporary, and I would have expected the text to drift back to its original position. Sorcery was like running a marathon—you needed to pace yourself. Sprint too early, and you could find yourself in trouble near the finish line. Moobin must have been feeling confident to tie off the end of the spell so the effect would be permanent. I looked under the car and noted that the gearbox was shiny like new and didn't have a leak. It looked like Lady Mawgon was having a good day too.

"Quark."

"Where?"

The Quarkbeast pointed one of his razor-sharp claws toward the east as Prince Nasil streaked past much faster than he should have. He banked steeply, circled the house twice, and came in for a perfect landing right next to us. He liked to carpet standing up like a surfer, much to the disdain of Owen of Rhayder, who sat on his carpet in the more traditional cross-legged position at the rear. Nasil wore baggy shorts and a Hawaiian shirt, too, which didn't go down well with Lady Mawgon.

"Hi, Jenny," said Nasil with a grin. "Delivery for you." He handed me a flight log to sign as the Quarkbeast wandered off.

At the front of the carpet was a large Yummy Flakes cereal box, which opened to reveal a tall and gangly lad with curly sandy-colored hair and freckles that danced around a snub nose. He was wearing what were very obviously hand-me-down clothes. He stared at me with the air of someone recently displaced and still confused over how they should feel about it.

Tiger Prawns

"H"ello," I said, holding out a hand. "I'm Jennifer Strange."

"They speak well of you back at the orphanage," he replied cautiously, shaking my hand as he climbed from the box. "I'm pleased to meet you. My name's Horton Prawns. Most people call me Tiger."

"Can I call you Tiger?"

"I'd like that."

He gave me a shy smile. He would have been twelve, the age I'd been when I joined Kazam. Like me, he would be a foundling brought up by the Lobsterhood, or to give the sisters their official title, the Blessed Ladies of the

Lobster. Their convent was in what was once Clifford Castle, not far from the Dragonlands. Tiger held up an envelope.

"Mother Zenobia told me to give this to the Great Zambini."

"I'm the acting manager," I told him. "You better give it to me."

"A foundling is the acting manager of a House of Enchantment?"

"You're not the first to be surprised — and I'll wager not the last. The envelope?"

But Tiger wasn't so easily swung. "Mother Zenobia told me to hand it *only* to the Great Zambini."

"He disappeared," I replied, "and I don't know when he's coming back."

"Then I'll wait."

"You'll give the envelope to me."

"No, I'm —"

We tussled over the envelope until I plucked it from his fingers and tore it open. It was his declaration of servitude, which was little more than a receipt. I didn't read it, didn't need to. Tiger belonged to Kazam until he was eighteen years old, same as me.

"Welcome to Kazam," I said, stuffing the envelope into my bag, "where unimaginable horrors share the day with moments of confusing perplexity and utter randomness. To call it a madhouse would insult even the maddest of madhouses."

"Double weird with added weird?"

"Pretty much. You'll be fine. Compared to the Sisterhood, it's almost normal. How is old Zenobia these days?" The convent's mother superior was a craggy old ex-enchantress who was as wrinkled as a walnut and about as resilient.

"I'm sorry to report that she's stark staring bonkers," replied Tiger.

"No change, then."

"Listen," said Prince Nasil, "if you don't need me, I've got a kidney to deliver to Aberystwyth."

I thanked Nasil for bringing Tiger over, and he gave us a cheery wave, lifted into a hover, and then sped off to the west. I had yet to break the news to him or Owen that the live organ delivery contract would soon be coming to an end.

"Miss Strange?"

"Jenny."

"Miss Jenny, why did I have to stay hidden in a cardboard box for the trip?"

"Carpets aren't permitted to take passengers. Nasil and Owen transport organs for transplant these days—and deliver takeout."

"I hope they don't get them mixed up."

I smiled."Not usually. How did you get allocated to Kazam?"

"I took a test with five other foundlings," replied Tiger.

"How did you do?"

"I failed."

This wasn't unusual. A half-century ago Mystical Arts Management had been considered a sound career choice and citizens fought for a place. These days it was servitude only, like agricultural labor, hotels, and fast food joints. Of the twenty or so Houses of Enchantment that had existed twenty years ago, only Kazam in the Kingdom of Hereford and Industrial Magic over in Stroud were still going. The power of magic had been ebbing for centuries and with it, the relevance of sorcerers. Once a wizard would have had the ear of a king; now we were rewiring houses and unblocking drains.

"The sorcery business grows on you."

"Like mold?"

"Pretty much, but don't talk like that to the others. They were once mighty. You have to respect what they *were* rather than what they *are* if you're going to fit in, and you need to. Six years at Kazam can be an eternity with people you don't like. Don't start off on the wrong foot. The enchanters are a quirky bunch, and they can be so annoying you want to beat them with sticks, but you'll get to love them like family—like I do."

"Six years?"

"Six years. But time passes quickly here. It's the variety."

The phone bleeped again. It was Kevin Zipp, one of our pre-cogs, a breed of sorcerer who deals less with the here and now than with the will and if. He had told me he would call me at this time several days ago, but as usual with those able to see a hazy version of the future, he had been uncertain of precisely *why*. He seemed to know now.

"Can you get back to the Towers?"

I glanced up at the three sorcerers, who were concentrating hard doing nothing. "Not really. Why?"

"I've had a premonition."

"What kind?"

"A biggie. Full color, stereo, *and* 3-D. I've not had one of those for years. I need to tell you about it."

And the radiophone went dead, just as the Quarkbeast reappeared.

"So listen, Tiger—"

He had a look of abject fear and horror: eyes wide and staring, left leg shaking uncontrollably, and a strange strangled noise in his throat. I'd seen this reaction before.

"That's the Quarkbeast," I told him. "He may look like an open knife drawer on legs and just one step away from tearing you to shreds, but he's actually a sweetie and rarely, if ever, eats cats. Isn't that so, Quarkbeast?"

"Quark," said the Quarkbeast.

"He'll not harm a hair on your head," I said, and the Quarkbeast, to show friendly intent, performed his second-best trick: he picked up a concrete garden gnome in his teeth and ground it with his powerful jaws until it was powder. He then blew it into the air as a dust ring and jumped through it. Tiger gave a half smile, and the Quarkbeast wagged his weighted tail, which was sadly a little too close to the Volkswagen and added one more dent to the already badly damaged front fender.

Tiger gave a nervous laugh, then reached out to touch the Quarkbeast, who shivered in a contented manner — few people dared stroke a Quarkbeast.

I could see there were hundreds of questions going around in Tiger's head, and he really didn't know where to start. "What happened to the Great Zambini?"

"Officially it's plain 'Mr. Zambini' these days, now that magic has dropped so much," I told him. "He hasn't carried the accolade 'Great' for over ten years, although we still use it as a mark of respect."

"You don't have it for life?"

"It's based on power. See the one dressed in black over there?"

"The grumpy-looking one?"

"The *dignified*-looking one. Sixty years ago she was Master Sorceress the Lady Mawgon, She-Whom-the-Winds-Obey. Now she's just plain Lady Mawgon. If the background wizidrical power falls any further, she'll be plain Daphne Mawgon and no different than you or I. Watch and learn."

We stood there for a moment.

"The fat one looks as though he's playing a harp," said Tiger.

"He's the once-venerable Dennis Price," I told him testily, "and you should learn to hold your tongue. Price's nickname is Full. He has a brother named David, but we all call him Half."

"Whatever his name, he *still* looks like he's playing an invisible harp."

"We call it harping because the hand movements that precede the firing of a spell look like someone trying to play an invisible harp."

"I'd never have guessed. Don't they use wands or something?"

"Wands, broomsticks, and pointy hats are for the storybooks." I held up my index fingers. "These are what they use. We used to take out insurance on their fingers in the old days, but we can't afford it now. Can you feel that?"

The faint buzz of a spell was in the air: a mild tingling sensation, not unlike static electricity. As we watched, Price let fly. There was a crackle in the air, and with a tremor, the entire internal wiring of Mr. Digby's house, complete with all light switches, sockets, and fuse boxes, swung out of the house—a three-dimensional framework of worn wiring, cracked Bakelite, and blackened cables. It hung in midair over the lawn, rocking slightly. Price had managed to do something in an hour that trained electricians would have taken a week to do, and he hadn't even touched the wallpaper, drunk any tea, or not turned up on Tuesday, as electricians do.

"Well held, Daphne," said Price.

"I'm not holding it," said Lady Mawgon. "I wasn't ready. Moobin?"

"Not I," he replied, and they looked around to see who else might be keeping the wiring levitated. And that's when they saw Tiger.

"Who's this little twerp?" asked Lady Mawgon as she strode over to us.

"The seventh foundling," I explained. "Tiger Prawns. Tiger, this is Full Price, Wizard Moobin, and Lady Mawgon."

Price and Moobin gave him a cheery hello, but Lady Mawgon was less welcoming.

"I shall call you F-7 until you prove yourself worthy," she remarked imperiously. "Show me your tongue, boy."

Tiger, who to my relief was quite able to be polite if required, bowed and stuck out his tongue. Lady Mawgon touched the tip with her little finger and frowned.

"It's not him. Mr. Price, I think you've just *surged*."

"You do?"

And the sorcerers fell into one of those very long and complex conversations that enchanters do when they want to discuss the arts. And since it was in Aramaic, Latin, Greek, and English, I could only understand one word in four—to be honest, they probably could too. Yet they did seem to have decided that there had been a surge of wizidrical power.

"Tongue in, Tiger," I said. "I have to go back to Zambini Towers," I called to the sorcerers. "Will you be okay here on your own to finish the job?"

They said they would, and after nodding to the Quarkbeast, who jumped into the back of my Volkswagen, Tiger and I left them to get on with it.

THREE

Zambini Towers

S o what are my duties?" asked Tiger as soon as we were on our way.

"Did you do any laundry at the Sisterhood?"

He groaned audibly.

"There's that, and answering phones, and general running around. I'm glad you're here, to be honest. Since we lost the fifth foundling two years ago and Zambini last year, I've been doing everything on my own."

"Everything?"

"Except the cooking. We have Unstable Mabel to do that for us, and you'll be glad to hear that washing the dishes is handled by spell. Stay out of her kitchen, by the way. Mabel has a nasty temper and is a deadly shot with a soup ladle."

"Can't the sorcerers do their own laundry?"

"They could, but they won't. Their power has to be conserved to be useful. And the retired ones have hardly any power left at all."

"Can't we use the dishwashing spell to do the laundry?"

"It was written in the ancient RUNIX spell-language," I explained, "and is read-only and can't be modified."

"Oh. Do I have to be called F-7 by the grumpy one?"

"You'll get used to it. It's better than 'Hey, you.' She called me F-6 until only a month ago."

"I'm not you. And besides, you still haven't told me what happened to Mr. Zambini."

"Later," I said, turning up the radio. I didn't want to talk about Mr. Zambini's disappearance. At least, not yet.

Twenty minutes later we pulled up outside Zambini Towers, which had once been the luxurious Majestic Hotel. It was the second tallest building in Hereford after King Snodd's parliament but was not so well maintained. The gutters hung loose, the windows were grimy and cracked, and moss was growing in the gaps between the bricks.

"What a dump," breathed Tiger as we trotted into the lobby.

"We can't really afford to bring it back to a decent state. Mr. Zambini bought it when he was still Great and could conjure up an oak tree from an acorn in a weekend."

"That one there?" asked Tiger, pointing at a sprawling oak that had grown in the center of the lobby, its gnarled roots and boughs elegantly wrapping around the old reception desk and partially obscuring the entrance to the abandoned Palm Court.

"No, that was Half Price's third-year dissertation."

"Will he get rid of it?"

"Fourth-year dissertation."

"Can't you just *wizard* the building back into shape or something?"

"It's too big, and remember, they have to conserve wizidrical energy. There's not much left."

We walked through the lobby, which was decorated with trophies, paintings, and certificates of achievements long past. Two elderly women were on their way to the breakfast rooms. They were dressed in matching tracksuits and cackled quietly to themselves.

"Good morning, ladies. This is Tiger, the new foundling," I said. "Tiger, these are the Sisters Karamazov — Deirdre and Deirdre."

"Why do they have the same name?" Tiger whispered.

"An unimaginative father."

The sisters looked very carefully at Tiger and prodded him several times with long bony fingers.

"Ha-ho," said the less ugly of the two, "will you scream when I stick you with a pin, you little piglet, you?"

I caught Tiger's eye and shook my head, to say they didn't mean anything.

The sisters looked at me. "You'll educate him well, Jennifer?"

"To the best of my ability."

"We don't want another . . . foundling incident."

"No, indeed."

And they hobbled off, grumbling to each other about the problem with spaghetti.

"They used to earn good money on weather prediction," I told Tiger as soon as they were out of earshot, "a skill now relegated to little more than a hobby after the introduction of computerized weather mapping. Don't stand next to them outside. A lifetime's work in weather manipulation has made them very attractive to lightning. In fact, Deirdre has been struck by lightning so many times it has addled her brain, and I fear she may be irredeemably insane."

"Winsumpoop bibble bibble," Deirdre called back as they vanished into the dining room.

"What did she mean by a foundling incident? Is that about the fifth foundling?"

"You'll find out."

"I don't think I'll be here long enough."

But I was confident that he wouldn't quit. For all the shortage of funds, bad plumbing, peeling wallpaper, erratic incantations, and dodgy spells, Kazam was *fun*. The sorcerers spent much of their time talking fondly about the good old days, telling tales of past triumphs and disasters with equal enthusiasm. The days when magic was powerful, unregulated by government. When even the largest spell could be woven without filling out the spell release form B1-7G.

"I'll show you to your room, Tiger."

We walked down the corridor to where the elevators had once been. They hadn't worked for as long as anyone could remember, and the ornate bronze doors were wedged open, revealing a long drop to the basement below.

"Shouldn't we take the stairs?" asked Tiger.

"You can if you want. It's quicker to just shout out the floor you want and hop into the elevator shaft."

Tiger looked doubtful, so I shouted, "Ten!" and stepped into the void. I fell upward to the tenth floor and stepped out as soon as the fall stopped. I waited for a moment, then peered down the shaft. Far below I could see a small face staring up at me.

"Remember to shout 'ten'!" I called down.

There was a terrified yell as Tiger fell toward me, which turned into a laugh as he stopped outside the elevator entrance. He struggled for a moment to get out, missed his moment, and fell back to the ground floor with a yell. When he fell back up to the tenth floor, I grabbed his hand and pulled him in before he spent the afternoon falling back and forth—as I had done when I first got here.

"That was fun," he said, trembling with fear and excitement. "What if I change my mind halfway?"

"Then shout it out and go to whatever floor you want. It's falling fast today. Must be the dry air."

"How does it work?"

"It's a standard ambiguity enchantment, in this instance, the difference between up and down. Carpathian Bob left it to us in his will. The last spell of a dying wizard. Powerful stuff. You'll be in room 1083. It's got an echo, but on the plus side, it *is* self-cleaning."

I opened the door to his room, and we walked in. The room was large and light and shabby. The wallpaper was stained and torn, the woodwork was warped, and unsightly damp patches had appeared on the ceiling. I *hoped* they were damp patches. I watched as Tiger's face turned into a smile, and he blinked away the tears. At the convent, he would have been used to sharing a dormitory with fifty other boys. To anyone else, room 1083 would have been a hovel — to the foundlings of the Sisterhood, it was luxury. I walked across to the window and removed the cardboard covering a broken pane, to let in some fresh air.

"The tenth floor is self-tidying," I said, "so nothing is ever out of place. Look."

I moved the blotter on the desk slightly off-kilter, and a second or two later it realigned itself. I then dug a handkerchief from my pocket and threw it onto the carpet. As soon as it hit the floor, it fluttered off to the top drawer of the bureau like a butterfly, folding itself as it went.

"Don't ask me how it works or who cast it, but be warned: enchantments have no intelligence. They follow spell subroutines without any form of discretion. If you were to fall over in here, you'd find yourself tidied away into the wardrobe, pressed and on a coat hanger."

"I'll be careful."

"Wise words. You can use the self-tidying feature, but don't *over*use it. Every spell is a drain on the power that runs through the building. If everyone were untidy, the speed of magic would slow dramatically. A handkerchief would self-fold in an hour, and the perpetual teapot would run dry. The same is true of the elevator. Play with it for too long, and it'll slow down and stop. I was stuck between floors once when Wizard Moobin was trying out one of his alchemy spells. Think of Zambini Towers as a giant battery of wizidrical power, constantly on trickle charge. If used a lot, it will soon run out. Used sparingly, it can go on all day. Is this room okay?"

"Do people knock when they want to use the bath?" he asked, staring into the marble-and-faded-gilt bathroom.

"Every room has its own bathroom," I told him.

He looked at me, astonished that such extravagance not only existed but would be offered to him. "A bed, a window, a bedside light, *and* a bathroom? It's the best room I'll ever have. I'm going to like it here, even with the weirdness and the laundry."

"Then I'll leave you to settle in. Come down to the Avon Suite on the ground floor when you're ready, and I'll tell you what's what. Don't worry if you hear odd noises at night. The floor may be covered with toads from time to time. Stay away from orbs. And never, *never* go to the thirteenth floor. Oh, and you must not look back if you ever pass the Limping Man in the corridor. See you later."

I was barely out the door when I heard a cry from Tiger. I looked back in.

"I saw a figure over there," he said as he pointed a trembling finger in the direction of the bathroom. "I think it was a ghost."

"Impossible—phantasms are confined to the third floor. You've just seen the echo I told you about."

"How can you see an echo?"

"It's not a sound echo, it's *visual*." I walked to the other side of the room, paused for ten seconds, and then walked back. Sure enough, a pale outline of myself appeared a few seconds later. "The longer you stay in one place, the more powerful the echo. We think it's a redundant strand on the self-tidying spell. Do you want to change rooms?"

"Are the other rooms any less weird?"

"Not really."

"Then this is fine."

"Good. I'll see you downstairs when you're ready."

Tiger looked around the room nervously. "Wait a moment while I unpack." He took from his pocket a folded necktie and placed it in one of the drawers. "I'm done."

And he followed me down the elevator shaft, but this time with a little more confidence, and a little less screaming.

FOUR

Kevin Zipp

"Can *you* do any magic?" Tiger asked as we walked past the shuttered ballroom on our way to the Avon Suite.

"Everyone can do a bit," I said, wondering where Kevin Zipp was. "If you're thinking of somebody and the phone rings and it's them, that's magic. If you get a curious feeling that you've been or done something before, then that's magic, too. It's everywhere. It seeps into the fabric of the world and oozes out as coincidence, fate, chance, luck, or what have you. The big problem is having enough magic to make it work for you in some useful manner."

"Mother Zenobia used to say that magic is like the

gold that is mingled in sand," observed Tiger, "worth a lot of money but useless if you can't extract it."

She was right. But if you have magic within you, are properly trained, and are the sort of person who can channel your mind, then it's possible a career in sorcery might be the thing for you.

"Were you tested?" I asked him.

"I was a 162.8."

"I'm a 159.3," I told him, "so we're pretty useless."

You have to have a thousand or more before anyone gets interested. You've either got it or you haven't — like being able to play a piano or go backwards on a unicycle while juggling seven clubs.

"You and me and Unstable Mabel," I added, "are the only nonmagic ones in the building."

"What about the Quarkbeast?"

"Magic through and through — one of a bunch of creatures created by the Mighty Shandar in the sixteenth century."

He looked down at the beast, who was trotting beside us while thoughtfully sucking the chrome off a section of car bumper he'd picked up somewhere.

"He was made by Shandar?"

"So they say. Here we are."

I opened the door to the Kazam offices and flicked on the light. The Avon Suite was large but seemed smaller due to a huge amount of clutter. There were filing cabinets, desks once occupied by long-redundant agents, tables, piles of paperwork, back issues of *Spells* magazine, several worn-out sofas, and in the corner, a moose. It chewed softly on some grass and stared at us laconically.

"That's the Transient Moose," I said, looking through the mail, "an illusion that was left as a practical joke long before I got here. He moves randomly around the building, appearing now and then, here and there. We're hoping he'll wear out soon."

Tiger went up to the moose and placed a hand on its nose. His hand went through the creature as though it were smoke.

I took the papers off a nearby desk and placed them on another, then pulled up a swivel chair and showed Tiger how to use the phone system. "You can answer from anywhere in the hotel. If I don't pick up, then you should. Take a message, and I'll call them back. "

"I've never had a desk," said Tiger, looking at the desk fondly.

"You've got one now. See that teapot on the sideboard over there?"

He nodded.

"That's the perpetual teapot. It's always full of tea. The same goes for the cookie tin. You can help yourself."

Tiger got the hint. I told him I liked my tea with half a sugar, and he trotted off.

"There are only two cookies left," said Tiger in dismay, staring into the tin.

"We're on an economy drive. Instead of an enchanted cookie tin that's always full, we've got an enchanted cookie tin with always only two left. You'd be amazed at how much wizidrical energy we save."

"Right," said Tiger, taking out the two cookies, closing the lid, and then finding two new cookies when he opened it again. "The economy drive explains why they're plain and not sweet."

"Quark."

"What is it?" The Quarkbeast pointed one of his sharp claws at a bundle of old clothes on one of the sofas. I went and had a closer look. It was the Remarkable Kevin Zipp, fast asleep and snoring quietly.

"Good morning, Kevin," I said cheerily. He blinked and stared at me, then sat up. "How is the job in Leominster?" I had found him some work in a flower nursery, predicting the colors of blooms in ungerminated bulbs. He was one of our better pre-cognitives, usually managing a success rate of seventy-two percent or more.

"Fine, thank you," muttered the small man. His clothes were shabby to the point of being rags, but he was exceptionally well presented in spite of it. He was clean shaven and washed, and his hair was fastidiously tidy. He looked like an accountant on his way to a costume party as a vagrant.

"This is Tiger Prawns," I said, "the seventh foundling."

Kevin took Tiger's hand in his and stared into his eyes. "Don't get in a blue car on a Thursday."

"Which Thursday?"

"Any Thursday."

"What kind of car?"

"A blue one. On a Thursday."

"Okay," said Tiger.

"So what's this about a vision?" I asked, sorting the mail. "We didn't finish our phone call."

"It was a biggie," Kevin began nervously.

"Oh, yes?" I returned equally nervously, having heard a lot of predictions that never came to anything, but some chilling ones that did.

"You know Maltcassion, the dragon?" Kevin asked.

"Not personally."

"Of him, then."

Everybody did. The last of his kind, he lived up in the Dragonlands not far from here, although you'd be hard-pressed to find anyone who could say they had caught a glimpse of the reclusive beast. I took the tea that Tiger handed me and placed the cup on my desk.

"What about him?"

Kevin took a deep breath. "I saw him die. Die by the sword of a Dragonslayer."

"When?"

He narrowed his eyes. "Certainly within the next week."

I stopped sorting the mail — mostly junk, anyway, or bills — and looked at Kevin Zipp, who was staring at me intently. The importance of the information wasn't lost on either of us. By ancient decree, a dragon's land belonged to whoever claimed it as soon as the dragon died, so there was always an unseemly rush for real estate that eclipsed a dragon's death. If Maltcassion were slain, within a day every square inch of land would be claimed. In the following months, there would be legal wranglings, then construction would begin. New roads, housing and power, retail parks and industrial units. All would cover the unspoiled lands in a smear of tarmac and concrete. A four-hundred-year-old wilderness would be gone forever.

"I heard that when Dragon Dunwoody died twelve years ago," said Tiger, "the crowd surge resulted in forty-seven people dead in the stampede."

Kevin and I exchanged glances. I felt something inside me turn over. The last dragon was a big deal, and it wasn't just about public safety or real estate. I didn't know quite how I knew, but I did.

"How strong was this vision?" I asked.

"On a scale of one to ten," replied Kevin, "it was a twelve. Most powerful premonition I've ever felt. It was as though the Mighty Shandar himself had called me up person to person *and* reversed the charges. I can detect it on low-alpha as well as the wider brain-wavelengths. I doubt I'm the only person picking this up."

I doubted it too. I phoned Randolph, Fourteenth Earl of Pembridge, the only other pre-cog on our books. Randolph, or EP-14 as he was sometimes called, was not only minor Hereford aristocracy but an industrial prophet who worked for Consolidated Useful Stuff (Steel) PLC, predicting failure rates on industrial welding.

"Randolph, it's Jennifer."

"Jenny, m'girl! I thought you'd call."

"I've got the Remarkable Kevin Zipp with me, and I wondered if—"

Randolph didn't need any prompting. He had picked up the same thing but could also furnish a time and date. Maltcassion would die next Sunday at noon. I thanked him and replaced the phone.

"Anything else?"

"Yes," replied Kevin. "Two words: Big Magic."

"Both capitalized?"

"Does it make any difference?" he asked.

"Certainly," I replied. "Lowercased big magic is simply magic that's, well, *big*. But Big Magic with capitals is something else entirely."

"Like what?" asked Tiger.

"I'm not sure," I replied. "Hence the 'something else entirely' comment. The sorcerers speak of it in hushed tones. I asked once, but I got stared at."

"By Lady Mawgon?" asked Kevin.

"Yes."

"I hate it when she does that," he murmured, and gazed at the worn linoleum, deep in thought. Being a precog wasn't a huge barrel of laughs. Generally speaking, you always got in trouble for not being specific enough. By the time the vision had been figured out, people were already dying.

"Before I go," he said, pulling a rumpled piece of paper from his pocket, "these are for you." He handed the grubby paper not to me, but to Tiger.

Tiger read the note as I looked over his shoulder. It didn't seem to mean anything at all.

Smith
91 and 11
Ulan Bator

"I don't understand," said Tiger finally.

"Me neither," shrugged Kevin. "Isn't seeing the future a hoot?"

Tiger looked at me, and I nodded that he should take it seriously.

"Thank you, sir," said Tiger with a bow.

"Well, there you have it," said Kevin, and left in a hurry, muttering that he had felt a good tip for Baron, a six-year-old mare running in the Hereford Gold Stakes Handicap.

The phone rang. I picked it up, listened for a few moments, and scribbled a note on a standard form. "This is a B2-5C," I told Tiger, "for a minor spell of less than a thousand shandars. I need you to take it up to the Mysterious X in room 245 and tell it that I sent you and that we need this job done as soon as possible."

He took the form and stared at me nervously. "Who, exactly, is the Mysterious X?"

"It's more of a *what* than a *who*. It won't be in a form you'll recognize, and there is something *other* about X that defies easy explanation. It's more of a sense than a person. A shroud, if you like, that confuses its true form. It also smells of unwashed socks and peanut butter. You'll be fine."

Tiger looked at the note, then at the Quarkbeast, then at where the moose had been but suddenly wasn't, then back at me. "This is a test, isn't it?"

He was smart, this one. I nodded. "You can be back with the Sisterhood by dinnertime, and no one will have thought any the worse of you. I'll let you in on a secret. You weren't sent to me as a punishment, nor by chance. Mother Zenobia is an ex-sorceress herself and only sends those she deems truly exceptional. Aside from the fifth foundling—the one we don't talk about—she's never been wrong."

"So was all that stuff about the Limping Man, the thirteenth floor, staying away from orbs, and being flown in a cardboard box also part of the test?"

"No, that was for real. And that's just the weird stuff I can remember right now. We haven't even started on emergency procedures yet."

"Right," Tiger said and, after taking a deep breath, left the room. He was back again a few moments later. "This job." He waved the form B2-5C nervously. "Is it something to do with Dark Forces?"

"There's no such thing. There are no 'Dark Arts' or 'wizards pulled to the dark side.' Misguided people can use magic for evil, but it's they who are wicked, not the magic. Magic, as I said, has no intelligence. The choice to use it for good or bad lies with us. All of us. And despite Zambini's absence, I will defend his goal to keep magic clean and uncorrupted!"

My voice had been rising, and Tiger, startled, took a step back. A teacup shattered on the sideboard, and I felt myself grow hot.

"Hang on," said Tiger. "I'm just the trainee."

"Sorry," I said, opening a window and taking a deep breath of cool air, "but doing Zambini's job isn't just about answering the phone and balancing the books."

Tiger laid a small hand on my arm. Foundlings looked after foundlings.

"You miss him, don't you?" he asked me.

"Like I miss my own father." I turned and blinked away the tears. Kevin's premonition about Dragondeath had rattled me more than I realized.

"I miss my father," said Tiger. "I don't know who he is, where he is, or whether he's alive or even knows I'm here — but I miss him."

"Me, too," I said, blowing my nose and thinking for a moment before clapping my hands together.

"Back to work. In answer to your question, Mysterious X's job is a cat stuck up a tree. It'll grumble, but it'll do it. Even inexplicable entities need cash to survive."

About the Mystical Arts

It was kind of . . . well, *vague*. Sort of shapeless — but with pointy parts."

"That's the Mysterious X all over," I said. "Did it show you its stamp collection?"

"It tried to," said Tiger, "but I was too quick for it. What exactly *is* the Mysterious X, anyway?"

I shrugged. There was a very good reason X carried the accolade *Mysterious*.

We were talking about the day over a prebedtime cup of hot chocolate in the kitchens. Wizard Moobin, Lady Mawgon, and Full Price had finished the rewiring job early and taken the bus back into town. They had been quite elated at the way the gig had gone, and even Lady Mawgon had permitted herself a small smile by way of celebration. Wizidrical power had been strong today—almost everyone had noticed it. I'd fielded a call from a journalist at the *Hereford Daily Eyestrain* with a question about Dragondeath. The premonition was getting around. I told her I knew nothing and hung up.

The rest of the afternoon had been spent explaining to Tiger how Kazam is run and introducing him to the least insane residents. He had been particularly taken with Brother Gillingrex of Woodseaves, who had made speaking to birds something of a specialty. He could speak Quack so well that he knew all eighty-two words ducks use to describe water. It turns out that birds worry endlessly about their appearance—all that preening is not only about flying, as they might have you believe—and a softly spoken "That looks *really* fetching and totally matches your plumage" works wonders.

"Does anyone else at Kazam have an accolade?" asked Tiger, who had realized that there was a lot to learn, and the sooner he got started, the better.

"Two Ladies, one Mysterious, three Wizards, one Remarkable, two Venerables, and a Pointless," I murmured, counting them off on my fingers, "but once upon a time, all forty-five had an accolade—and higher than the ones I've just mentioned."

"Who's the Pointless?"

"It would be impolite of me to reveal, but you'll probably figure it out for yourself."

"So those accoladed Wizard are the most powerful?"

"Not quite," I replied. "An accolade isn't based simply on performance but on reliability. Wizard Moobin isn't the most powerful in the building, but he's the most consistent. And to complicate matters further, a status is different from an accolade. Two wizards might both be status Spellmanager, but if one has turned a goat into a moped and the other hasn't, then the first gets to be called Wizard."

"A goat into a moped?!"

"You couldn't do that. It's just an example."

"Oh. So who decides who gets an accolade?"

"It's self-conferring," I replied. "The idea of any kind of organized higher authority — a Grand Council of Wizards or something — is ridiculous once you get to know how scatty they can be. Getting three of them to spell together is possible — barely — but asking them to agree on a new color of the dining room, almost impossible. Argumentative, infantile, passionate, and temperamental, they need people like us to manage them and always have. Two steps behind every great wizard has always been their agent, always taking a back seat but always there, doing the deals, sorting out transportation, hotel bookings, mopping up the mistakes and the broken hearts, that sort of thing."

"Even the Mighty Shandar?"

"There is no *record* that he had one, but we're usually the first to be written out of history. Yes, I'm almost certain of it. Imagine being the Mighty Shandar's agent. No percentage, but the fringe benefits would be colossal."

"Would you get dental insurance?"

"Tusks if you wanted them."

"Do you enjoy it?" he asked, and I had to think for a moment.

"Doing your duty is perhaps not the same as *enjoyment*," I said slowly, "but who would look after them if not me?"

"If I can last, I guess I will."

I stared at him. I'd be gone from here in two years, on my eighteenth birthday, and already I was dreading it.

"Do you have to leave?" he asked.

"It's when my indentured servitude is up," I said, "and I get the freedom to do what I want."

"What if what you want to do is work here?"

"Then I'll come back," I said thoughtfully, "but I want the freedom to make that decision for myself."

"I can't fault your logic," said Tiger, "so tell me more about accolades."

"Right. The one thing sorcerers are good at is honor.

You wouldn't award yourself an accolade that you didn't deserve, or shy from demoting yourself if your powers faded. They're good and honest people — just a bit weird, and hopeless at managing themselves."

"So what about the one who accoladed himself Pointless?"

"Self-confidence issues."

Tiger thought about this for a moment. "So what could a sorcerer do on the Spellmanager level?"

I took a sip of hot chocolate. "Levitation of light objects, stopping clocks, unblocking drains, and simple washing and drying can all be handled pretty well at the Spellmanager level. There's no one below this status at Kazam except you, me, Unstable Mabel, the Quarkbeast, and Hector."

"Hector?"

"Transient Moose." I nodded in the direction of the moose, who was leaning against one of the refrigerators with a look of supreme boredom. "Above this is Sorcerer. They can conjure up light winds and start hedgehog migrations. Sparks may fly from their fingertips, and they might manage to levitate a car. The next rank is that of Master Sorcerer. At this level, you might be expected to create objects from nothing. A light drizzle could be conjured up, but not on a clear day. Above this is Grand Master Sorcerer. These gifted people can levitate several trucks at a time, change an object's color permanently, and start isolated thunderstorms. They might be able to squeeze out a lightning bolt but not very accurately. The final category is Super Grand Master Sorcerer, who can do almost anything. He or she can whistle up storms, command the elements, and stop the tide. They can create spells and incantations that are so strong that they stay long after the wizard has died. They are also supremely, incredibly, thankfully, *rare*. I've never met one. There aren't any. Not now, anyway. The greatest of all the Super Grand Master Sorcerers was the Mighty Shandar. It was said that he had so much magic in him that his footprints would spontaneously catch fire as he walked."

"And the Mighty Shandar is where we get the base measurement of wizidrical power — the shandar?"

"That's about it."

"But there are others, surely? Out there, doing normal jobs, who have this power?"

"Several hundred, I imagine," I replied, "but without a license to practice, they'd have to be either very stupid or very desperate to start chucking spells around. To perform magic of any kind, you have to have a Certificate of Conformity — a license. Once that hurdle has been crossed, you have to be accredited to a licensed House of Enchantment. After that, each spell has to be logged on a form B2-5C for anything below a thousand shandars, a B1-7G form for spells not exceeding ten thousand shandars, and a Form P4-7D for those over ten thousand shandars."

"That would be a seriously big spell," said Tiger.

"Bigger than you and I will ever see. The last P4-7D job was signed off in 1947, when they built the Thames Tidal Barrage. There was a lot more power around in those days, but even so it took a consortium of twenty-six sorcerers, and the wizidrical power peaked at one-point-six megashandars. It was said the sand in children's sandboxes turned to glass within a twenty-mile radius. They evacuated the local area for a job that size, naturally."

"What if someone did?" Tiger asked. "Do an act of illegal sorcery, I mean?"

I took a deep breath and stared at him. "It's about the only thing the twenty-eight nations of the Ununited Kingdoms agree upon. Any unlicensed act of sorcery done outside the boundaries of a House of Enchantment is punished by . . . public burning."

Tiger looked shocked.

"I know," I said, "an unwelcome legacy from the fourteenth century and reinforced by the Blix episode in 1878. *Highly* unpleasant. And that's why you, me, we, *everyone* has to be extra diligent when filling out the forms. Miss something or forget to file it, and you're responsible for a good friend's hideous punishment. We lost George

Nash four years ago. A lovely man and a skilled practitioner. What he couldn't tell you about smoke manipulation wasn't worth knowing. He was doing a routine earthworm charming, and his B1-7G form wasn't filled in. Someone's eye wasn't on the ball."

Tiger tilted his head to one side. "It was the fifth foundling, wasn't it?"

Tiger really was smart. Mother Zenobia had sent us the best.

"Yes," I said, "but the fifth foundling's name isn't spoken under this roof."

We sat in silence, the only sound the panting of the Quarkbeast, the chewing of the Transient Moose, and the occasional sip, from us, of hot chocolate.

Tiger was probably thinking the same thoughts I was—about being a foundling. We had both been left outside the Convent of the Blessed Ladies of the Lobster before we were old enough to talk. We didn't know our true birth dates, and our names weren't the ones we were born with—the sisters named us. I think that's why Tiger had guessed that the fifth foundling was the one responsible for George Nash. There is no greater insult among foundlings than to refuse to acknowledge the one thing you value more than anything else: your name.

"Did you ever try to find out?" asked Tiger. I knew he meant my parents.

"Not yet," I replied. Some of us built them up and were disappointed; others built them down so they wouldn't be. All of us thought about them.

"Any clues?"

"My Volkswagen," I replied. "It was abandoned with me in it. I'm going to find out its previous owners when I get out of servitude. You?"

"My only clue was a weekday roundtrip ticket to Carlisle and a medal," replied Tiger, "placed in my basket when I was left outside the convent. It was a Fourth Troll Wars Campaign medal with a Valor clasp."

"*Lots* of parents were lost in the Troll Wars," I said.

"Yes," said Tiger in a quiet voice. "Lots."

It was getting late. I stretched and stood up. "Good first day, Tiger, thanks."

"I didn't do much."

"It's what you didn't do that matters."

"And what didn't I do?"

"You didn't run away screaming, or try to fight me, or make peculiar demands."

"I like to think the Prawns are like that," he said with a smile, "loyal and dedicated."

"How about fearless?"

He looked at the Quarkbeast. "We're working on that."

I saw him up to his room and told him where he could find me if he needed anything, and he said he was just fine, and everything was one hundred percent faberoo because he had his own room and that was the best thing ever, even if it was enchanted. The Quarkbeast at my heels, I went down to my room and brushed my teeth, then climbed into my pajamas, taking the precaution to lay out a blanket and pillow on the floor, just in case. I then took down the poster of Sir Matt Grifflon, singing star, as it made me seem a little undignified.

I had been reading in bed for only a few minutes when the door opened and Tiger tiptoed in, snuggled up in the blanket I had laid out, and sighed deeply. He'd never slept on his own before.

"Good night, Tiger."

"Good night, Jenny."

I turned off the light and lay awake for a while, my head full of dragons, premonitions, and, for some reason, destiny. But not the ultimate destiny of magic that everyone at Kazam worried about. The destiny that disturbed me was *mine*.

SIX

The Magiclysm

Tiger was gone by the time I awoke. The Quarkbeast, too, so I imagined he had communicated to Tiger that he liked to take a walk in the back alleys behind the paper mill, where his fearsome appearance wouldn't send anyone into traumatic shock. I knew the Quarkbeast well, and he sometimes frightened even me. It is said that the only thing a Quarkbeast looks good to is another Quarkbeast, but they never gather in pairs, for a reason I wasn't quite sure about.

I took a quick bath, dressed, and stepped out of my room. I was on the third floor, sandwiched between the room shared by the Sisters Karamazov and Mr. Zambini's suite. I noticed a sharp sensation in the air, very similar to the tingling that precedes a spell. The lights flickered in the corridor, and my bedroom door, which I had closed behind me, slowly swung open. I felt the building shimmer and the tingling sensation grow stronger, and then, one by one, the light bulbs fell from their fittings, bounced on the carpet, and rolled to the far end of the corridor. Beneath my feet, I could feel the floorboards start to bend, and several toads dropped from nowhere.

I needed no further warnings. Zambini had briefed me about a *Magiclysm*. I ran to the alarm next to the elevator, broke the glass, and pressed the large red button.

The klaxon sounded in the building, warning all those within to use whatever countermeasures they could. Almost immediately the misters filled the entire hotel with a fine dampness, which felt like stepping inside a cloud. Water is an ideal moderator and is about the only thing that can naturally quench a spell that is about to go critical. A few seconds later there was a tremendous detonation from somewhere upstairs. The tingling and vibrations abruptly stopped, and I turned to see a cloud of plaster and dust descend the stairwell. I switched off the alarm and ran up the stairs — elevators, even enchanted ones, should never be used in an emergency. I found Wizard Moobin lying in a heap on the fifth-floor landing.

"Moobin!" I exclaimed as the dust began to settle. "What on earth happened to you?"

He didn't answer. Instead, he clambered unsteadily

to his feet and returned to his room, the door of which had been blown clean off its hinges and was now embedded in the opposite wall. I stared through the doorway at the devastation. A wizard's room is also a laboratory, as all sorcerers are inveterate tinkerers by nature and may spend entire lifetimes in pursuit of a specific spell to do a specific job. Even something as inconsequential as the charm for finding a lost hammer had taken Grendell of Cleethorpes a lifetime to weave in the twelfth century. A destroyed workshop often indicated several decades of important work lost in one short blast of uncontrolled wizardry. Magic can be strong stuff and bite the unwary.

I followed Wizard Moobin into his room and trod carefully through the jumbled wreckage. Most of his books had been destroyed, and all the carefully laid-out glassware, retorts, and flasks had been reduced to shards. But Moobin seemed curiously unconcerned; nor was he worried that his clothes had been blown off him, and he was now dressed only in a pair of underpants and a sock.

"Are you okay?" I asked, but the wizard was far too busy searching for something to answer. I exchanged glances with Half Price, who had arrived at the door. Despite being identical twins born two weeks apart, he and Full Price were hardly alike at all. Half was thin and Full was stout.

"Wow!" said the Youthful Perkins, who had also just arrived. "I've never seen a spell go critical before. What were you doing?"

"I'm fine," Wizard Moobin muttered, turning over a broken tabletop. I picked up a fire extinguisher and put out a small fire in one corner of the room.

"What happened?" I asked again, and Moobin suddenly stood up from where he had been searching in a pile of smoldering papers. With a shaking hand, he passed me a small toy soldier. It had only one leg, carried a musket, and was very heavy. It was made of pure gold.

"Yes?" I asked, still in the dark.

"Lead, used to be, was, like, at least. Then, well—" exclaimed the wizard excitedly, trying to find a chair undamaged enough to sit on.

"You're babbling," I told him.

"Lead—now—gold!" he said at last.

"Way to go!" said the Youthful Perkins enthusiastically. He had been joined by the Sisters Karamazov, who were jostling each other for the best view.

"Lead into gold!?" I repeated incredulously, knowing full well that such a spell requires a subatomic meddling that is almost unheard of below a Grand Master Sorcerer. "How did you manage to do that?"

"That's the interesting thing," replied Moobin. "*I have no idea.* Every morning I concentrate my mind on that lead soldier, summon up every shandar in my body, and let fly. For twenty-eight years nothing has happened, not a flicker. But this morning—"

"Big Magic!" yelled the younger Karamazov sister.

Wizard Moobin looked up abruptly. "Do you think so?"

"Rubbish," returned the other sister. "Don't listen to her—she's one spell short of a curse."

"I was more powerful than usual in the rewiring job yesterday," Moobin said thoughtfully. "Perhaps the surge is sustaining for a bit longer."

This, I mused, was possible. It could just be an ordinary surge; the background wizidrical power was subject to periodical fluctuations. I was disconcerted to hear about Big Magic again, but for now there were practical matters to consider.

"I hate to be a stickler for regulations," I said, "but you're going to have to fill out a form B2-5C for this. I know we're in the Towers, but we should stay on the safe side. We'd better do a P3-8F as well, just in case."

"P3-8F?" queried Moobin. "I haven't heard of *that* one before."

"Experimental spells resulting in accidental damage of a physical nature," put in the younger Karamazov sister, who despite the repeated lightning strikes could still have moments of lucidity.

"I see," replied Moobin, turning to me. "If you fill them in, I'll sign them."

I left him to tidy up and walked downstairs to the ground floor, where I met Tiger and the Quarkbeast returning from their walk. Tiger had a graze on his nose, his clothes were scuffed, and he had some twigs in his hair.

"If he starts to run, you have to drop his leash as soon as possible," I advised.

"I know that now."

"Did he drag you far?"

"It wasn't the distance," replied Tiger, "it was the terrain. What's going on?"

"Wizard Moobin experienced a surge," I said as we entered the offices in the Avon Suite. I sat down at my desk and pulled the *Codex Magicalis* toward me so I could make sure I didn't need to fill out any more paperwork. "Something's going on. Yesterday they finished the rewiring in record time, and this morning Moobin turned lead into gold."

"I thought the power of magic was diminishing."

"It is. But every now and again it surges upward, and they can all do things they haven't been able to do for years. The problem is that surges usually herald a slump, and if you couple this with what Kevin Zipp told us yesterday, we could find ourselves without magic at all come next Sunday."

"You think dragons have something to do with magic?"

"It was one of Zambini's many theories," I replied. "He said there must be a reason Kazam is based in the Kingdom of Hereford. We're twenty miles away from the Dragonlands, and while a link between dragons and magic has never been proved, there's more than enough anecdotal evidence to link the two. In any event," I added, "if we're to try and preserve the mystery and majesty of magic, we need to find out more."

We sat in silence for a moment.

"By the way," said Tiger, "is the Quarkbeast allowed to crunch up corrugated iron before breakfast?"

"Only galvanized," I replied without looking up. "The zinc keeps his scales shiny."

After the excited buzz about Moobin's accident died down and everyone had tried the lead-into-gold thing themselves without any success, I got down to the day-to-day running of Kazam. I had a job for Full Price — to divine the location of a wedding ring that had been flushed accidentally down the toilet — and another tree-moving job that Patrick of Ludlow could handle. I sorted through the mail. There were a few checks, so our accountant would be happy, although I didn't want to see him because he assumed I knew all about accounting, which I didn't — I had taken cooking instead of the class that included double-entry bookkeeping. There was another letter; this one carried the official seal of the Hereford City Council, and it informed me that our contract to clean the city's drains would not be renewed. I called my contact at the council to find out why.

"The fact is," said Tim Brody, acting assistant deputy head of drains, "Blok-U-Gon has undercut your price, and we have a budget to think of."

"I'm sure we can come to some arrangement," I said, trying to act as Mr. Zambini might. Some work we did at a loss, simply to keep the sorcerers busy or to give us a presence in the marketplace. We needed the public to see us working in order to gain their trust and promote wizardry as normal—even mundane.

"Listen," I said, "a drain cleared by magic is the best way. It doesn't smell, there's no fuss, you don't have to be embarrassed by what you blocked it up with, and besides, I offer a good guarantee. If it blocks again within twenty-four hours, we redo the job for free and charm the moles from your garden—or your face. The choice is yours. I even do the form B1-7Gs for you. Besides, it's traditional."

"It's not just the cost, Jennifer. My mother used to be a sorceress, so I've always tried to use you guys. The problem is that King Snodd's Useless Brother recently bought a five percent share in Blok-U-Gon, and—well, you see?"

"Oh," I said, realizing that this was bigger than both of us. "Right. Thanks, Tim. I'm sure you did your best."

I hung up. Although King Snodd IV was in general a fair and just ruler who seldom put people to death without good reason, he was not averse to making edicts that were of financial interest to him and his immediate family. There was nothing I could do. He was the king, after all, and indentured servitude or not, I and all those who held Hereford nationality were loyal subjects of the crown.

"We just lost the drain unblocking contract to King Snodd's Useless Brother," I told Tiger.

"I don't know anything about his Useless Brother, but Mother Zenobia took us all to see King Snodd on Military Hardware Parade Day," remarked Tiger thoughtfully.

"What did you think?"

"The landships were impressive."

"Quark."

The door to the office cracked open, and a large man in a sharp suit and a fedora peered in. He soon noticed the Quarkbeast. Hard not to, really.

"Does it, er . . . bite?"

"Never deeper than the bone."

He jumped.

"Just a joke, Mr. — ?"

The large man looked relieved and entered. He removed his hat and sat in the chair I offered him while Tiger was dispatched to fetch a cup of tea.

"My name is Mr. Trimble," announced the man, "of Trimble, Trimble, Trimble, Trimble, and Trimble, attorneys at law." He handed me a card. "That's me there," he said, helpfully pointing to the third Trimble from the left.

"Jennifer Strange," I replied, handing him a brochure and rate card.

There was a pause. "Can I speak to someone in charge?"

"That's me."

"Oh!" he said apologetically. "You seemed a little young."

"I'll be sixteen in two weeks," I said, "and I've been at Kazam for four years, the acting manager for six months. You can talk to me."

"Commendable, Miss Strange, but I usually speak to Mr. Zambini."

"Mr. Zambini is regrettably . . . unavailable right now."

"Where is he?"

"*Indisposed*," I replied firmly. "How can I help?"

"Very well," said Mr. Trimble. "I represent the Consolidated Useful Stuff Land Development Corporation. Do you have any reliable pre-cogs on your books?"

"I have two," I answered, glad for the additional work, and from someone who could pay their bills — the Consolidated Useful Stuff Land Development

Corporation was the property arm of Consolidated Useful Stuff, and there wasn't much that ConStuff didn't do and own. They even had their own kingdom in the chain of islands to the east of Trollvania, which used a large foundling labor force to make cheap and shabby goods far more cheaply and shabbily than anyone else—a clear advantage that allowed them to dominate the Ununited Kingdoms' cheap and shabby goods market.

It was said that of every spondoolip, dollop, acker, or moolah spent in the Ununited Kingdoms, one in six went into ConStuff's pocket. No one much liked them, but few didn't shop there. ConWearStuff had recently introduced an "all you can wear for five moolah" section, and on my miserable allowance, I couldn't afford to shop anywhere else. To my credit, I *did* feel guilty afterward.

"Two pre-cogs?" said Trimble, taking a checkbook from his pocket. "That's excellent news. I wonder if any of them have predicted the death of the loathsome Maltcassion recently?"

I hoped he didn't see me flinch. "Why?"

"Well," continued Mr. Trimble genially, "it's just that my aunt had a vision last night of the dragon's death."

"Did she say when?"

"No—this year, tomorrow, who knows? She's only rated a 246.3, so her predictions are a bit wild. But I can't ignore it. All that land ripe for claiming. Knowing the precise time of the dragon's death in advance would be invaluable to a property developer, if you get my meaning. Land is so much better managed when there is one company administering it. Having the general public own dribs and drabs here and there and everywhere can be highly irksome, wouldn't you agree?"

He smiled and handed me a check. I gasped. It was for two million Herefordian moolah. I'd never seen so many zeros in one place without "overdrawn" written next to them.

"If you can tell me the precise time and date, I will return and sign that check. But *only* for the correct time and date. Do you understand?"

"You . . . want to cash in on the death of the last dragon?"

"*Precisely* what I mean," Trimble said happily, mistaking my annoyance for agreement. "I'm so glad we understand each other."

Before I could say another word, he had shaken my hand and walked out the door, leaving me staring at the check. His offer would clear our overdraft and quite possibly send all the wizards into a cozy retirement—and retirement was always a possibility, given the diminishing power of magic.

"By the way," he said, popping his head back through the doorway, "there seems to be a moose in the corridor."

"That would be Hector," said Tiger. "He's transient."

"Perhaps so," replied Trimble, "but he's blocking the way."

"Just walk through him," I said, still deep in thought, "and if you've ever wanted to know how a moose works, stop halfway and have a good look around."

"Right," said Mr. Trimble, and left.

I leaned back in my chair. The word of Maltcassion's apparent demise was getting around. Such things are not to be treated lightly. And when I'm in need of advice, there is only one place to go: Mother Zenobia.

SEVEN

Mother Zenobia

The convent of the sacred order of the Blessed Ladies of the Lobster had once been a dank and dark medieval castle but was now, after a lick of paint and a few throw pillows, a dank and dark convent. The building overlooked the River Wye, which was pleasant, and it was right on the edge of the demilitarized zone, which wasn't. Successive King Snodds had looked upon the Duke of Brecon's neighboring duchy with envious eyes, and a garrison from each had faced each other across the ten-mile strip of land that was their only shared border.

The upshot was that King Snodd's artillery was behind the convent and fired a daily shell over the building, to fall harmlessly into the demilitarized zone beyond. The Duke of Brecon, whose saber rattling had recently been reduced to dagger rattling due to a cut in his defense budget, had his artillerymen yell "bang" in unison in reply, and he reserved live shells for special occasions, such as birthdays.

Despite the standoff on their doorstep, the Sisterhood grew and supplied the city with vegetables, fruit, honey, and foundlings in exchange for cash, which allowed them to continue to bring up orphans like me and Tiger. To the foundlings, the artillery camped out in the orchard was of singular unimportance, except that you could tell the time by the single shot, which was always at 8:04 precisely.

I parked my Volkswagen outside the convent, and the Quarkbeast and I walked silently through the old gatehouse in an attempt to surprise Mother Zenobia, who was dozing in a large chair on the lawn. She was well over one hundred and fifty but still remarkably active. A Troll War widow, she had taken to the Lobsterhood soon after the loss of her husband. There were hushed rumors of a former riotous life, but all I knew for sure was that she had held the 1927 air-racing record in a Napier-engined Percival Plover at 208.72 MPH. I had seen the trophy commemorating the feat in her small room — even Ladies of the Lobster are permitted one small vanity.

"Jennifer?" Mother Zenobia asked, reaching out a

hand for me to touch. "I saw you drive up. Is your car orange?"

"It is, Mother," I replied.

"And you are wearing blue, I think?"

"Right again," I replied, amazed. She had been totally blind for nearly half a century.

She clapped her hands twice and bade me sit next to her. A novice ran up, and Mother Zenobia ordered her to bring me some tea and cake, then tickled the Quarkbeast under the chin and gave him her own teacup and saucer to crunch, which is a bit like waving your hand near an open food blender with your eyes closed. The Quarkbeast had never given me any trouble, but the sight of his knifelike fangs could still unnerve me.

"How is young Prawns settling in?"

"Very well. He's answering the phones as we speak."

"A special one," remarked Mother Zenobia, "and destined for great things, even if a bit troublesome. He managed to pick the lock of the food cupboard no matter how many times we improved security."

"I didn't see him as a thief."

"Oh, he never stole anything—he just did it to demonstrate that he could. He'd read the entire library by the time he was nine."

She paused for a moment, then said, "Tiger's father was third engineer on a landship in the Fourth Troll War. Vanished during the Stirling Offensive."

The offensive had been simply one more campaign against the trolls, in order to push them back into the far north. For this, the Ununited Kingdoms had put aside their differences and assembled eighty-seven landships, war machines as big as a five-story building. Powered by four vast diesel engines and built of riveted iron, their wide tracks could propel them through a town, flatten a forest, and cross the widest river without so much as pausing for breath. The landships had passed the first Troll Wall at Stirling and arrived at the second Troll Wall eighteen hours later. The last radio contact came shortly after they had opened the Troll Gates, and then—nothing. The generals had ordered the infantry to advance rapidly to the front to "assist where possible," and not one of them was ever seen again.

The final toll of those "lost or eaten in action" was close to a quarter million men and women. The first Troll Wall was rebuilt, and plans for the invasion of the troll territory postponed.

"But," continued Mother Zenobia, "only tell Tiger when he asks."

"I'll be sure to."

"Is this a social visit?" she asked.

"No," I confessed.

"Then it's about the Dragondeath."

"You can feel it, too?"

"Given the power of the transmission, there won't be

anyone who hasn't by the end of the week. Has anyone mentioned Big Magic recently?"

"They have. What is it?"

"All in good time. What is your interest in dragons, young Jennifer?"

"I'm not sure." I shrugged. "But something's not right."

Mother Zenobia chuckled enigmatically. "It is time," she said in a grand manner. "Master Prawns isn't the only one destined for great things. You are too. And to that end, you need to know more about dragons."

I frowned. Zambini thought dragons were linked to magic, but I didn't see how that had anything to do with me. I didn't do magic, I *managed* it, and there's a big difference.

But I knew better than to argue with Mother Zenobia, and maybe she would tell me something that would help Kazam's business. She began.

"Dragons, like four o'clock tea, crumpets, marmalade, and zip-up cardigans, are a peculiarity to the Ununited Kingdoms. They are fierce, fire-breathing creatures of great intelligence, dignity, and sensitivity who could and did converse on matters of great importance. But for all their intelligence, wit, and social graces, dragons still had one habit that made them impossible to ignore."

"And that is?"

"They liked to eat people."

"I thought that was just a story to frighten children."

"Oh no, it's true all right," replied Mother Zenobia sadly, "they did. And don't interrupt. For centuries these islands had an uneasy peace with the dragons. Since dragons didn't like crowds and favored feeding at night, it was best to stay indoors and avoid going for long walks on your own. If you did, then it was wise to wear a large spiked helmet of copper, something dragons find highly unpalatable.

"But for all these precautions, dragons *did* still eat people, and the country lived in fear. Four or five hundred years ago, knights were the only method of dragon-slaying, and many a fearless young knight, driven by the promise of a king's daughter's hand in marriage, would boldly sally forth to attempt to kill a dragon, returning—he hoped—with the jewel that a dragon had in its forehead as proof of the conquest.

"The problem was, not many managed to kill a dragon. Indeed, out of a recorded 8,128 attempts by knights, only twelve managed to succeed, mostly due to a lucky charge with a brave horse and a providential jab in the unarmored section just beneath the throat. After two hundred years, interest in becoming a knight and marrying a princess started to wane, and following the time when five knights tried a multipronged attack and were all returned impaled on a lance like a giant kebab, knights were forbidden from dragonslaying, which caused a great deal of relief, but generally only among the knights."

"What happened then?"

"For two hundred years, not much. Even the discovery of gunpowder failed to make a dent in the dragon population. Cannonballs just bounced off a dragon's hide, giving it nothing more than indigestion and a sore temper. Many a thatched village was set on fire by a dragon who had been annoyed at being shelled when he was sunning himself quietly in the afternoon.

"The only solution to the Dragon Problem seemed to be the use of magic. But since dragons are fine practitioners of the sacred arts themselves, it required the arrival of a magician so utterly powerful that it was said his footprints spontaneously caught fire as he walked—"

"The Mighty Shandar?"

"Right. No one knew where he came from, nobody knew where he went, and few people even know what he looked like or what he liked to eat. But in one respect everyone was agreed: the Mighty Shandar was the most powerful magician the planet had ever known. Greater than Mu'shad Waseed, the Persian wizard who could command the winds. More powerful than Garance de Povoire, the French Wizard of Bayeux, or even Angus McFerguson, the Scottish sorcerer who made the Isle of

Wight a floating isle that could be towed by tugs to the Azores for the winter and, to the best of my knowledge, still is."

"I think they have engines attached to it now," I mentioned. "Did . . . did the Mighty Shandar have an agent?"

"History does not record one. Why do you ask?"

"No reason. What happened next?"

Mother Zenobia paused for thought.

"It was in June 1591. As soon as the Mighty Shandar arrived, he demonstrated his awesome powers and promptly built the Great Castle at Snodd Hill, which has housed the ruling kings of Hereford ever since. He sat in his castle and waited for the word to spread. And spread it did. Within a week, ambassadors from the then seventy-eight different kingdoms of Britain descended on the Great Castle, all to offer him employment.

"But the Mighty Shandar was not a man to take sides. He would work for none of them, but *all* of them. So the seventy-eight ambassadors went away and had consultations with their leaders and one another and reported back to the Mighty Shandar that the greatest thing he could do would be to deal with the Dragon Problem. Shandar put his great fingers to his great forehead and thought great thoughts; he agreed to the great task, but because of the great difficulty and the great amount of time it would take, he would require a great deal of money. Eighteen dray-weights of gold.

"'Eighteen dray-weights of gold?' the ambassadors said to one another, shocked at so high a price. 'Are you nuts? Mu'shad Waseed offered to rid us of the dragons for only seven dray-weights!'"

"The Mighty Shandar *definitely* had an agent," I said with a smile, "and better than Mu'shad Waseed's."

"Didn't I tell you not to interrupt?"

"Sorry."

Mother Zenobia continued. "'But Mu'shad Waseed,' replied Shandar in answer to the ambassadors, 'fine magician as he is, does not have in his entire body one hundredth the power I have in my smallest toe.'

"'I heard that!' said Mu'shad Waseed, throwing off his disguise and stepping forward. He had secretly arrived at Shandar's palace the day before, having heard of Shandar's demands. 'Let's see this mighty toe of yours!'

"But instead of showing Mu'shad Waseed his toe, the Mighty Shandar bowed so low that his forehead touched the ground, and he said, in a voice toned deep with respect and reverence, 'Welcome to my humble palace, most noble Wizard of the Persian Empire, controller of the winds and tides and known locally as He Who Can Quell the Tamsin.'"

"Don't you mean Khamsin," I asked, "the hot and dusty wind that blows through the Arabian Peninsula?"

"If I *meant* Khamsin, I would have *said* Khamsin," replied Mother Zenobia. "Tamsin was Mu'shad Waseed's second wife. Frightful, *frightful* woman. Her love of glittery things, fine robes, and bathing in rabbit's milk set feminism back four centuries."

She continued. "'Great Mu'shad Waseed,' said Shandar, 'I read of your work in *Spells* magazine. Your control of the thunderstorms and the winds is quite awe-inspiring.'

"But Mu'shad Waseed, who was the combustible mix of a Persian father and a Welsh mother, was too angry to return Shandar's politeness and instead caused a massive rainstorm to move in from the west, and as all the ambassadors of the seventy-eight kingdoms of the Ununited Kingdoms ran for cover, Mu'shad Waseed and Shandar faced each other. Their eyes narrowed, and a Super Grand Master Sorcerer's contest seemed ready to begin. But Shandar, whose turn it was by the sorcerers' code to begin the contest, did nothing.

"'You may deal with the Dragon Problem,' said Shandar slowly, a smile gathering on his lips. 'I shall return when you fail.' And so saying, he vanished.

"Mu'shad Waseed gulped. In reality, he knew that his power was puny compared to that of the Mighty Shandar. Building his castle in Alexandria had taken him not one night but a month. Although he had, on occasion, built palaces during a lunch break, none had included — as Shandar's did — a four-acre heated swimming pool, a library containing every book ever published, and a zoo that featured most of the world's animals and a few that the Mighty Shandar had made up himself, the Quarkbeast among them.

" 'Whoops,' thought Mu'shad Waseed, as the seventy-eight ambassadors of the Ununited Kingdoms emerged from their carriages wearing raincoats and galoshes, eager to know how Mu'shad Waseed was going to deal with the Dragon Problem."

EIGHT

The Dragon Problem

D espite his misgivings," Mother Zenobia continued, "Mu'shad Waseed accepted the task and threw himself heartily into the project. His first act was the instigation of a class of warriors known as Dragonslayers, men and women who were bold in heart and soft in the head, sworn into service after a five-year apprenticeship. To each of these hundred Dragonslayers was given a sword, a horse, a home, and an apprentice who would learn from his master. All seemed well, and Mu'shad Waseed sent his Dragonslayers to slay the dragons.

"Initially, things seemed to go pretty well. Reports came flooding in of defeated dragons, and the number of jewels plucked from the foreheads of the dragons rose quickly. Since the census of the day listed forty-seven active dragons, the ambassadors of the Ununited Kingdoms wanted to see forty-seven jewels as proof that the Dragon Problem had been solved. Mu'shad Waseed was not the only person eager to see the seven dray-weights of gold. Besieging the Persian wizard's camp were representatives of hoteliers and restaurateurs, laundry companies and tailors, who had all given Mu'shad Waseed eight years of credit and now wanted their money. As reports of fallen dragons came pouring in, parties were planned throughout the islands by the grateful inhabitants; a land without dragons meant their harvest wouldn't be burned, their livestock wouldn't be eaten, and they could walk around at night without wearing an uncomfortable copper helmet. So everyone, for the moment, was happy.

"When Mu'shad Waseed announced that all the dragons had been slain, the seventy-eight ambassadors brought the gold to pay him in many stout carts drawn by oxen. There was a celebratory banquet, but then, after the speeches but before the liqueurs, a fierce whooshing, beating of wings, and growling came from the north. In the dying light of the day, the party guests could see the sky darken with the approach of the dragons: keen on the wing, lively on the claw, and breathing fire while howling an agonizing war cry. The party ceased; the musicians stopped playing. The milk turned sour, and the wine turned to vinegar. There could be no doubt that the dragons were converging on the feast of Mu'shad Waseed.

"The revenge of the dragons was quick, terrible, and absolute. Mu'shad Waseed, his magic weakened by his eight years of toil, could do nothing, and the terrible screams of the lizards and their victims were heard twenty miles away.

"Only one person was spared to relate the story," said Mother Zenobia. "It was said that Mu'shad Waseed was enveloped in a thunderous blast of fire so intense that he was turned to charcoal where he stood. The dragons razed Mu'shad Waseed's headquarters until all that was left was a fine gray ash. Then the dragons vanished, leaving behind a blackened patch of earth and a lot of disgruntled hoteliers and restaurateurs who, as far as we know, never did get paid.

"Mu'shad Waseed had failed. The dragons carried on as before. Unsurprisingly, they reacted badly to the attempted extermination and caused much trouble on the islands; the Dragonslayers could do little. By the time snow once more blanketed the land, only three dragons had been slain to seven lost Dragonslayers. It was a disaster, and the seventy-eight kings, emperors, queens, presidents, dictators, dukes, and elected representatives who had paid Mu'shad Waseed to do not very much fiercely regretted not spending the extra eleven dray-weights of gold and employing the Mighty Shandar instead."

"That's quite a story," I said as Mother Zenobia stopped for breath, "but if there were still dozens of dragons, where did the forty-seven forehead jewels come from?"

"No one knows," replied Mother Zenobia. "Perhaps the dragon census was inaccurate, or Waseed decided to claim his reward by making false jewels. But that's not the best part."

She paused for a moment, then produced a pair of pliers from the air and plunged them into the Quark-beast's open mouth.

"Sister Angeline had a Quarkbeast," she said, panting slightly with exertion. "A pair of pliers, a corkscrew, and an angle-grinder should be included in the grooming kit. Ah—got it!"

She withdrew the pliers as the Quarkbeast shut his jaws with a snap. Held in the pliers was a piece of twisted metal.

"Tin can. Just behind the fifth canific molarcisor. Common problem. Where was I?"

"You were about to tell me the best part."

Mother Zenobia smiled. "This: the Mighty Shandar did not return that winter. He did not return that spring. Summer turned to autumn, turned back to summer, and then to spring again. And then one day, the following summer after *that*, Shandar reappeared.

" 'Sorry I'm late,' he said, once all the ambassadors had gathered before him. 'I had one or two things to attend to.'

" 'You *must* help us,' begged the ambassadors, all of whom were new but one, 'Mu'shad Waseed tried to create Dragonslayers, but now the Dragon Problem is worse than ever — '

" 'I know, I know,' interrupted the Mighty Shandar. 'I read all about it in the papers. Frightful business. My price for peace with the dragons is now *twenty* drayweights of gold. Do you accept?'

"After a brief conversation, the seventy-eight ambassadors accepted unconditionally, and Shandar got to work.

"In the first year, he learned to speak Dragon. In the second year, he learned where the dragons held their annual general meeting. In the third and fourth years, he attended the meetings, and in the fifth, he spoke.

" 'Oh, dragons wise and bountiful,' he said, although we have only his word for what happened, as no one accompanied him. 'The humans seek my help in destroying you, and I could do precisely that.'

"Here he turned the dragon next to him to stone, to demonstrate.

" 'Paltry human!' scoffed Earthwise, the elected head of the Dragon Council. 'Watch this!'

"But try as he might, not even the finest magic of the strongest dragon could turn their comrade back from stone again. Nor could they attack Shandar, as he had woven a force of electricity between himself and the dragons, and anyone who came close got their claws zapped. When they had calmed down, Shandar changed the stone dragon back to life and said, 'Mankind will not be puny mortals forever. I can see a time when the cannonballs they annoy you with will be as nothing; great land creatures made of iron will crawl up to your lairs and blast you with cannons more powerful than you can possibly imagine. After that I see winged creatures of steel flying faster than sound itself. I can see all this in the future and say to you now that peace needs to be made with the humans.'

"Earthwise looked at him, a wisp of smoke escaping his nostrils and floating to the roof of the cave. He could see parts of the future, too, and he knew that Shandar spoke the truth. They talked long into the night, and then the following morning Earthwise bore Shandar to the seventy-eight ambassadors, who listened eagerly to the plan that had been drawn up.

"It was very simple. The dragons were to have lands given over to them. The lands would be kept stocked with sheep and cows for them to eat. Each Dragonland would be surrounded by boundary stones protected by a strong magic that would vaporize a human if he or she tried to pass. The dragons agreed to give up eating people and stop torching villages, and to leave townsfolk's cattle and sheep well alone. The sole remaining Dragonslayer would keep an eye on things to ensure fairness, and if a dragon transgressed the laws, the Dragonslayer would mete out any punishment.

"And so it was agreed. The Dragonlands were established, stocked with livestock, and marked with boundary stones. The Dragonslayer was reeducated in her new role as peacemaker, and Shandar took his twenty dray-weights of gold. And that," concluded Mother Zenobia with a dramatic flourish, "is the story of the Dragonpact."

"And what happened to the Mighty Shandar?" I asked.

"That was four hundred years ago. The Mighty Shandar went into semiretirement in Crete. The number of dragons has been diminishing ever since. All but one has died of old age. Since Dragon M'foszki died eleven years ago, Maltcassion, who still resides in the Dragonlands not ten miles from here, is the last of his breed. When he goes, the dragons will be no more."

"But what about — ?"

But Mother Zenobia had vanished into a gray mist;

abrupt teleportation was just one of her many skills. I looked at the convent behind me and could see her rematerialize in the dining room. Today's lunch must have been sausages, her favorite.

With my mind full of dragons and pacts and Shandars and slayers and marker stones and lunch, which I had forgotten to eat, I drove up to the Dragonlands. I parked and walked across the turf to the humming marker stones, which encircled the lands at twenty-foot intervals, and looked around.

On the Dragonlands side of the stones, the countryside was pristine unspoiled moorland. On the human side, it was a different story. Tents and campers had sprung up everywhere, now that the word had spread that Maltcassion was about to go belly up. Small groups of people talked while seated on folding chairs, sipping tea from thermos flasks. Everyone seemed to have a good supply of tent pegs and string with which to make their claim, and with the Dragonlands covering an area of almost 350 square miles, a lot was at stake. Several enterprising souls had even parked their Land Rovers pointed in toward the lands, ready to bounce into the interior and claim as large an area as they could.

As Mother Zenobia had said, the previous dragon to die had been M'foszki, the Great Serpent of Bedwyn, whose lair had been on the Marlborough downs. Quite suddenly the marker stones had stopped humming, and every square inch had been claimed within twenty-four hours.

I stared into Maltcassion's empty Dragonlands, then at the people who were still arriving at the border, following the call of cash as if they had some deep-rooted herding instinct. The milk of human kindness was turning sour.

NINE

Patrick and the Childcatcher

Tiger was in the lobby when I got back to Zambini Towers, and I asked him why he wasn't manning the telephone as he had been told.

"Very funny," he said.

"I see you've met Patrick of Ludlow," I replied, trying to stifle a giggle, for Tiger was thirty feet up in the shabby atrium, perched high upon a chandelier. "How long have you been up there?"

"Half an hour," he answered crossly, "with only a lot of dust and Transient Moose for company."

"You'll have to take a few jokes in good humor," I told him, "and consider yourself lucky that you have witnessed both passive and active levitation in the same day."

"Which was which?"

"Carpeteering is active; heavy lifting is passive. Could you feel the difference?"

Tiger crossed his arms sulkily. "No."

"Did your metal fillings ache when he lifted you?"

"My fillings are marzicrete," he replied grumpily. "They were cheaper."

"Never mind." I walked off toward the Kazam offices. "I'll ask Patrick to get you down."

Our heavy lifter was eating cookies in the Avon Suite when I arrived. Patrick of Ludlow was a year shy of his fortieth birthday, amiable if a little simple, and quite odd-looking. Like most sorcerers who made their living using passive levitation, he had muscles mainly where he shouldn't — grouped around his ankles, wrists, toes, fingers, and the back of his head.

"How did the clamping removals go?" I asked.

"Eight, Miss Jennifer, which brings my score to four thousand, seven hundred and four. The most popular car color for people who don't care where they park is silver; the least popular, black."

"Was it Wizard Moobin who told you to put Tiger up there?" I knew he wouldn't have done it on his own.

"Yes, Miss Jennifer. Was that wrong of me?"

"No, it was just a joke. But get him down now, okay?"

Patrick waved his hand in the direction of the lobby, and a minute or two later Tiger walked back into the office with a scowl.

"Patrick, this is Tiger Prawns. Tiger is the seventh foundling, here to help me run the place. Tiger, this is Patrick of Ludlow, our heavy lifter, who was told to put you up there by wizard or wizards unknown and is thus blameless. You will be friends and not hold a grudge."

Patrick jumped up politely, said how happy he was to meet Tiger, and thrust out a hand for him to shake. Tiger blinked. The hand looked like a joint of boiled ham with fingertips poking out the end, and I watched to see what he would do faced with an appendage so misshapen. To his credit, he didn't flinch and instead held one of the fingertips and shook that. The lack of any reticence pleased Patrick, who grinned broadly — although he'd come to terms with the way he looked, he'd never really gotten used to it.

"Sorry about putting you up there," he said.

"No problem." Tiger had become more cheery now he knew the prank wasn't malicious. "The view was very pleasant. How do you hold things with hands like that?"

"I don't need to," replied Patrick, and demonstrated by raising his tea to his lips by thought power alone.

"Useful," said Tiger. "Who was the person on the *other* chandelier?"

"What?"

Tiger repeated himself, and we went out to the lobby to check. When I saw, I had to bite my lip to avoid giggling.

"Patrick," I shouted down the corridor, "would you let the Childcatcher down, please?"

Patrick reluctantly let the man down, but not as lightly as he had Tiger, and the truant officer landed heavily on the carpet.

"Sorry about that," I said, even though I wasn't, "but Patrick has a long memory, and you and he didn't get along, did you?"

"It's an unpopular profession," said the Childcatcher, brushing himself off, "but someone must do it." He had a weasely face covered in unsightly pustules, framed between two curtains of lifeless black hair. "He should show greater respect to a servant of the crown."

"And he will," I assured him. "We take any disrespect to King Snodd's representatives most seriously."

"Good," said the Childcatcher, although I could tell he wasn't wholly convinced. "I understand you have a new foundling, and I want to know why he has not been enrolled in any schools."

Tiger and I exchanged glances. He'd be too busy for school, and working at Kazam was education enough.

Besides, if he *did* need to learn anything truly academic, we could always get one of the wizards to help. A book hidden under an enchanted pillow at night works wonders. Sadly, the school board didn't see it that way.

"Unless I have a very good reason for Master Prawns's nonattendance, we shall be forced to send him to school against his will."

I didn't know what to say. Mr. Zambini had bribed the Childcatcher when he came for me, but that had been a different childcatcher—one who had eventually gone to prison for taking bribes. Luckily for me, school became optional for foundlings at age fourteen—I think it was something to do with economics and the cheap labor supply. I wasn't sure bribery would work with this one even if we had some money, which we didn't, and using sorcery to bend the will of a civil servant was not just a one-way ticket to the pyre but unethical.

"I don't need to go to school," said Tiger confidently, "because I already know everything."

I frowned at his sweeping statement, but the Childcatcher laughed and said, "Then answer me this: What did the S stand for in General George S. Patton?"

"Was it Smith?"

"Hmm," said the Childcatcher suspiciously, "probably a lucky guess. What are the two prime factors of one thousand and one?"

"Easy. Eleven and ninety-one."

I stifled a laugh and attempted to look serious as Tiger reeled off the answers that the Remarkable Kevin Zipp had given him only that morning. It was just as well he had memorized them.

"Okay, that was quite impressive," said the Childcatcher. "Final question. What is the capital of Mongolia?"

"Is it Ulan Bator?"

"It is," replied the Childcatcher uneasily. "Looks like you are what you say you are. Good afternoon, Master Prawns. Good afternoon, Miss Strange." And he stomped angrily from the hotel.

"Well," said Tiger, "I know now why Kevin Zipp carries the accolade Remarkable. How does he do at the races? I expect he makes a fortune."

"He's lost every penny he ever owned," I replied, "and the shirt off his back. Soothsayers are like that. They see many futures, but never their own."

Norton and Villiers

I closed up the office at five after completing the form P3-8F for Wizard Moobin's accident and all the B1-7Gs for the day's work. Once each was signed by the magician it related to, my day was done. But as I walked along the corridor toward the lobby, the Quarkbeast's hackles rose, and he made growly Quarky noises deep in his throat. It was easy to see why. There were two men waiting for me beneath the spreading boughs of the oak tree.

"Call the Quarkbeast off, Miss Strange," said one of the men. "We're not here to harm you or it."

The men were well dressed and very familiar. They

were royal police and were always the ones assigned to investigate any possible deviation from the Magical Powers (amended 1966) Act. I'd known them for as long as I had been here, and two things were certain: (1) they would go away empty-handed, and (2) they always began with the same introduction, even though they knew exactly who I was — and I them.

"I'm Detective Villiers," said the taller and thinner of the two, "and this is Sergeant Norton. We work for the king, and we would like you to help us with our inquiries."

Villiers was a good deal heavier than Norton, and we often joked in the office that they looked like the before and after in a diet advertisement.

The Quarkbeast sniffed Villiers's trouser leg excitedly and wagged his tail.

"You have a new prosthetic leg, Detective," I observed, "made of magnesium alloy."

"How did you know?"

"Magnesium is catnip to a Quarkbeast. If you still have your old one, I'd wear it next time you come round."

"I'll remember that," he said, peering nervously at the Quarkbeast, who was in turn staring intently at his leg, his razor-sharp fangs dripping with saliva. He'd have eaten the leg in under a second if I'd allowed him, but Quarkbeasts, for all their fearsome looks, are obedient to a fault. They are nine-tenths velociraptor and kitchen blender and one-tenth Labrador. It was the Labrador tenth that I valued most.

"So, gentlemen," I said, "how can I help?"

"Is Mr. Zambini back yet?" asked Villiers.

"I'm afraid not."

"I see. You have soothsayers and pre-cogs on your books, I understand?"

"You know I have," I answered, "and they both hold Class IV premonition certificates."

"Quark," said the Quarkbeast.

"Have any of your pre-cogs mentioned the death of Maltcassion?" asked Norton.

"It doesn't take any special skills, Sergeant. Take a look up at the Dragonlands. Besides, doesn't the king have a seer of his own?"

Villiers nodded. "He certainly does. The Inconsistent Sage O'Neons has predicted the death of the dragon but also mentioned that the dragon was to be killed by a Dragonslayer. Does this sound correct?"

"No one can enter the Dragonlands *but* a Dragonslayer, Villiers. I think perhaps Sage O'Neons is less astounding than you think."

"Insulting the king's advisors is an offense, Miss Strange."

I'd had enough of all the beating-around-the-bush stuff. "What do you want, Villiers? This isn't a social call."

Villiers and Norton exchanged glances. The door to the Palm Court on the other side of the lobby opened, and the Sisters Karamazov popped their heads in.

"I'm fine, sisters, thank you." They nodded and withdrew. Villiers spoke next.

"Sage O'Neons said a young woman named Strange would be involved in the Dragondeath."

"There must be hundreds in the phone book."

"Perhaps, but only one has a Quarkbeast." The Quarkbeast looked up quizzically.

"Quark," he said.

The officers stared at me as though I were somehow meant to account for why I'd appeared in one of the royal seer's visions. In any other circumstances, I could have ignored them, but with everything that was going on, I was beginning to wonder — no matter how impossible that sounded.

"Pre-cogs," I began, not wanting to give anything away, "even *royal* ones, don't always get it right. Any seer worth his salt will tell you a premonition is seven-tenths interpretation. And remember, Strange isn't just a name. It's an adjective."

Villiers and Norton shuffled uneasily. It probably didn't make a whole lot of sense to them either, interviewing someone on the basis of a vision, but when the king spoke, they had to do his bidding.

"We're just following a number of leads, Miss Strange. I hope you consider your allegiance to His Majesty King Snodd IV (may he live forever) above all else?"

"Of course."

Villiers nodded. "Then I would expect a call if you knew anything?"

"Goes without saying."

They knew I didn't mean it, and I knew they knew. They bade me good afternoon and left, purposefully leaving the front door open.

I went up to my room and switched on the television. It was as I had feared: the news was going national. The Ununited Kingdoms Broadcasting Corporation was running a live feed from the Dragonlands—they had even sent their star anchorwoman.

"This is Sophie Trotter of the UKBC," announced the reporter, "speaking live from the Maltcassion Dragonlands, here in the Black Mountains. A wave of premonitions about the death of the last dragon has given rise to a gathering in the Marcher Kingdom of Hereford. No one can say for sure when this event will happen, but as soon as the repulsive old lizard kicks the bucket, the good people of the Ununited Kingdoms can finally sleep easily in their beds, secure in the knowledge that the last of these loathsome worms has been eradicated from the world. The question on everyone's lips is: When? An answer that we, as yet, do not know. But when the dragon finally croaks, you can be sure that UKBC will be in with the first wave of new claimants of the land. Next up, an exclusive interview with leading Herefordian knight Sir Matt Grifflon, who explains why the dragon needs to die and performs his latest hit song, 'A Horse, a Sword, and Me.'"

"Makes you sick, doesn't it?" said a voice from the door. It was Wizard Moobin, none the worse for the explosion that morning.

"Sir Matt Grifflon's new song?" I asked. "No, I thought it was quite good—if you like that kind of thing."

"The Dragonlands. If I had my way, I'd make them a national park, a safe haven for wild Quarkbeasts. Isn't that right, lad?"

"Quark," said the Quarkbeast happily. I gave him two unopened tins of dog food. He crunched them up happily, cans and all.

"We agree on that," I replied, "but if you're going to play jokes on the new boy, can you please not ask Patrick of Ludlow to help out? He's very impressionable."

"I don't know what you mean. Watch this."

He put out his hand and narrowed his eyes. There was a crackle in the air, and a vase displaced itself from my dresser and flew across the room to his outstretched hand. The Quarkbeast quarked excitedly—there was now a bunch of flowers in the vase as well.

"These are for you," said Moobin gallantly, presenting the roses with a flourish.

I took the flowers carefully, for they were just images conjured up by the wizard. They twinkled with small sparks of electricity in the dimness of the room and changed colors slowly, like the setting of the sun. They were beautiful but wholly out of Moobin's league.

"They're fantastic!" I muttered, adding, "Don't think me rude, but—"

"I'm as surprised as you are," he confessed, pulling a small device from his pocket. It was a portable shandarmeter, a device for measuring wizidrical power. He turned the gadget on and handed it to me. I pointed the meter at him as he levitated the vase.

"What did I get?" he asked.

"Nine hundred twenty shandars."

"Last week I could barely manage five hundred," said Moobin excitedly. "Even if we discount the lead/gold switcheroo as a surge, I'm still twice as powerful as I was two days ago."

"You think it's connected with the Dragondeath?"

"A definite link between dragons and magic was never proved, but the nearer I am to the Dragonlands, the stronger my powers. The same jobs I might try in London take a lot more effort. I rarely like to work much farther than Yorkshire, yet my father was powerful as far away as the Great Troll Wall."

"The Great Zambini always thought it was due to dragons," I observed. "More dragons, more magic. Fewer dragons, less magic."

"We often wondered," said Moobin thoughtfully. "When Maltcassion dies, does magic go with him? All this might be the last knockings — the brief surge an engine will give before it runs out of gas."

"Sister Karamazov mentioned Big Magic," I said. "What did she mean?"

Moobin thought for a moment. "It's an old wizard's legend — a massive burst of wizidrical power that changes everything."

"Good or bad?"

"Either, neither, or both. No one knows."

We stood in silence. I needed to know more. The future of Kazam might depend on it.

"Perhaps if I were to talk to the Dragonslayer?" I ventured.

"Is there one?"

"There *has* to be, doesn't there? It was part of the Dragonpact."

"You could try. It's possible that the dragon may not

die. After all, seers and pre-cogs only see a *version* of the future. There are few premonitions — if any — that can't be altered."

After Wizard Moobin left, I gazed at the roses, which twinkled and faded as the magic wore off. Owen of Rhayder knocked on my door soon after. He was our second carpeteer. Owen had defected to Hereford from the ramshackle Cambrian Potentate in mid-Wales about ten years earlier, which isn't hard to do if your particular skill is carpet.

"Look at this, Jennifer girl," he said crossly, unfurling the carpet and letting it hover in the middle of the room. "There's mangy for you."

He waved a lamp under the carpet, and the light gleamed through the threadbare old rug. "As soon as a hole opens up, I'm going to retire. I don't want to go the way of Brother Velobius."

Brother Velobius had run a magic carpet taxi service about thirty years ago, in the days before all sorts of regulations seriously hampered the carpet business. On a high-speed trip to Norwich, Brother Velobius and both his passengers had died when his Turkmen Mk18-C Bukhara carpet broke up in midair. The Air Accident Investigation Department painstakingly rebuilt the carpet and eventually concluded that the breakup was caused by rug fatigue. All carpets were vigorously tested after that, and when none passed the stringent safety rules for passenger carrying, they were relegated to solo operation and delivery duties. But that wasn't all: operators were told to carry licenses, a registration number, navigation lights for night flying, and a mandatory upper speed limit of one hundred knots. It was like selling someone a Ferrari and telling the new owner not to change out of first gear.

"It looks like we're going to lose the live organ transportation contract," I told Owen.

His face fell, and he lowered the carpet to the floor, where it rolled itself automatically and hopped into the corner, startling the Quarkbeast, which dived under the table in fright.

"So it's pizza and curry deliveries, then?" he asked bitterly.

"We're in negotiations with FedEx to make up the shortfall."

"Deliveries aren't the *spirit* of carpeting, Jenny *bach*," he said sadly. "Organ delivery made us *relevant*."

"I'm really doing my best, Owen."

"Well, perhaps your best is not good enough."

He glared at me, unfurled his carpet, and was off out of the window, streaking back toward Benny's Pizza to do some deliveries.

ELEVEN

Mutiny

I'm not paying," announced Mr. Digby angrily, waving the bill I had hurriedly written out for the rewiring and replumbing job. "I specifically said *plastic* piping."

It was the following morning, and Mr. Digby had turned up as soon as Tiger and I opened the office.

"We don't work in plastic," announced Full Price.

"We don't work in plastic," I repeated.

"Listen," said the man. "If I ask a plumber to re-plumb the house, and I specify plastic, then that's what you'll use. I pay the bills, I call the shots."

"If you understood how sorcery works," I said, "you would know that long chain polymers do not react as well—"

"Don't try and blind me with your voodoo science!"

"Very well," I said with a sigh. "I'll instruct my people to remove all the plumbing immediately."

"No, you won't!" said Mr. Digby angrily. "If I catch you on my property, I'll call the police!"

I stared up at the red-faced man and wondered whether the sorcerer's code of ethics couldn't be relaxed for just a moment; I thought our irate customer would make a fine warthog. "I'll meet you halfway."

Mr. Digby grumbled as Price rose in disgust and walked out the door.

"The more you do this," I said, altering the total on the bill and recalculating the tax, "the fewer sorcerers there will be to do this sort of work. The next time you want any plumbing done, you'll have to get a builder in and tear all the plaster off the wall."

"What do I care?" sneered Mr. Digby. "The job is done." He stormed out, and Full Price came back in. Price wasn't very happy.

"It took us only half a day to do his house, Jennifer. An army of plumbers couldn't do it that fast, and I got a splitting headache to boot. We should have taken him to court."

I got up and placed the check in the cash box. "You know as well as I do, the courts rarely side with the Mystical Arts. All he has to do is invoke the 1739 Bewitching Act, and you could end up on a dunking stool—or something worse. Is that what you want?"

Full Price sighed. "I'm sorry, Jennifer. It just makes me so mad."

The phone rang, and Tiger picked it up. "Hello, Kazam Mystical Arts Management. Can I help you?" He paused. "No, I'm sorry, madam, we can't turn people into toads. It's usually permanent and highly unethical . . . No, not even for cash. Thank you."

At that moment, Lady Mawgon strode in with Moobin close behind. She didn't look too happy—furious, actually.

"I've explained about Mr. Digby to Full Price," I said, feeling mildly nervous. Mr. Zambini had been gone six months, and although I had so far avoided any arguments, they would eventually happen—and as likely as not, from Mawgon.

"We're not here about that," said Lady Mawgon, and I noticed several other Zambini Towers residents at the door. Some were on the active list, like Kevin Zipp, and others not, like the Sisters Karamazov. There were also ones I hadn't seen for a while, long-retired eleventh floorers such as Monty Vanguard the Sound Manipulator and an old and very craggy sorceress who looked as though she were half tortoise.

"What can I help you with, then?"

"Am I to understand," began Lady Mawgon, trembling with indignation, "that Mr. Trimble of the Con-Stuff Land Development Corporation offered Kazam two million moolah for the precise time of the Dragondeath?"

"He did, and I said I'd think about it."

"Isn't that the sort of decision that we should *all* make, in the absence of Mr. Zambini?" asked Lady Mawgon.

"Two million moolah is a lot of moolah," added Price.

"And could pay for *all* our retirements," put in Monty Vanguard.

"I'm not sure the deal is still on the table," I said, trying to stall for time.

"Mr. Trimble contacted me," said Lady Mawgon. "The deal is *definitely* still on."

"Listen," I said, suddenly hot all over, "we don't know for sure the Dragondeath is going to happen. The link between magic and dragons is not proven, but there's not a sorcerer in the building who doesn't believe it exists. There's a whiff of Big Magic in the air, and I don't think we should be cashing in on the Dragondeath — it's just not what we do."

"Who are you to decide what we do?" demanded Lady Mawgon imperiously. "Try as you might, you cannot be Mr. Zambini, and never will be — you are simply a foundling who got lucky." Several of the other sorcerers winced. None of them would have gone *that* far. Lady Mawgon was making it personal.

"If he's going to die anyway, it's free cash," remarked Full Price, trying to calm the situation down, "and if the Big Magic goes the wrong way, we'll have lost out completely—no magic, no cash. And if the enchantment holding up this building unravels, no home either."

"The way through is clear," announced Lady Mawgon, even though it wasn't. "You must give us Mr. Trimble's check and the time and date of the Dragondeath."

But I wasn't yet finished.

"We all know how premonitions work," I said, swallowing my anger about the foundling jab, "and they'll sometimes come true only because we expect them to. If we sell the time and date to Trimble, then the dragon may die whether he was meant to or not. If Big Magic goes the wrong way, as Price suggests, then we may have exchanged magic for cash. I'm not sold on that, and I think many of you will agree. Everyone is here at Zambini Towers because of what they are or what they have been. And I think that counts for something."

There was a pause. Sorcerers like money as much as the next person, but they like honor and their calling better. Ask a wizard if they'd swap their powers for a sack of cash, and they'll choose magic every time.

"This is all conjecture," remarked Monty Vanguard.

"What in sorcery isn't?" added Half Price. "I'm with Jennifer on this one."

"There's no conjecture in a cozy retirement guaranteed," said the half tortoise from the eleventh floor, speaking for the first time.

We all stood in silence for a moment, so I thought I should act. I took Trimble's unsigned check from the cash box and laid it on the desk.

"Dragondeath Sunday at noon," I said, feeling a thumping pulse in my temples. "As Lady Mawgon has so graphically pointed out, you don't need me to make the decision for you, and no, I'm not Mr. Zambini, and we don't know when or if he's coming back. But as long as my name is Jennifer Strange, I won't help ConStuff profit by Maltcassion's death. And what's more," I went on, my anger suddenly making me impetuous, "you can find a new acting head of Kazam if you do. I'll work out the rest of my servitude helping Unstable Mabel and mucking out the Mysterious X when he has another one of his episodes."

There was silence when I'd finished, and they all looked at one another uneasily.

"I think we should put it to a vote," said Moobin.

"There won't be a vote," said Lady Mawgon, reaching for the check. "Our path has never been so clear."

"Touch that check without a vote, and I'll newt you," said Moobin.

It was quite a threat. Being changed into a newt is a spell a wizard will use only as a last resort. It is irreversible and, technically, murder. But Lady Mawgon thought he was bluffing. After all, it takes a lot of power to newt someone.

"Your days of newting were over long ago," she said.

"Lead into gold, Lady Mawgon, lead into gold."

Wizard Moobin and Lady Mawgon stared at each other. Spells were never instantaneous and required a modicum of hand movements. The thing was, whoever made the first move was the aggressor. If you moved first and newted someone, you were a murderer. Move last, and it was self-defense. There was silence in the room as the two of them stared at each other, hardly daring to blink. A week ago this would have been a hollow threat, and even though neither of them had newted anyone for decades, the increased background wizidrical energy and the fact that it was early morning meant that such a thing was possible.

The Remarkable Kevin Zipp broke the standoff. "No one's going to newt anyone."

Mawgon and Moobin looked mildly relieved at Zipp's pronouncement. After all, neither of them wanted to be a murderer — the punishment is particularly nasty.

"How strong was the premonition?" I asked Kevin.

"Oh, it wasn't a premonition," he confessed with a grin. "I was just listening in to Master Prawns's phone conversation." No one else had been paying attention to Tiger. We all turned as he placed the handset back on its cradle.

"That was the news desk at the UKBC," he said. "I just told them the time and date of the Dragondeath."

"You did *what*?" demanded Lady Mawgon, turning bright red.

He repeated himself to a shocked silence from the room, and then added, "Now the information is out in public, so ConStuff has no advantage. The deal is dead."

"You shouldn't have done that," remarked Wizard Moobin.

"Well, I did," Tiger said, taking a deep breath. "You can newt me if you like, but Jenny is right. Dragons are noble creatures and as likely as not the source of your power. It would be like selling your index fingers. My conscience is clear."

"I'll make you wish you'd never been born!" screeched Lady Mawgon, and pointed a long bony finger in his direction.

Tiger didn't even blink. "I'm a foundling," he said simply. "I often wish I'd never been born."

Lady Mawgon paused, lowered her finger, and then

strode from the room with a loud cry of "Foundlings, bah!" The others filed out soon after, glaring daggers at Tiger as they went, until only he and I were left.

"That was a stupid thing to do," I said. "Stupid but brave."

"You and me both, Miss Strange. You were going to resign over it, and I wasn't going to let that happen."

He stared up at me with a look of hot indignation. Mother Zenobia had been right. This one was special. I couldn't be angry with him, but I couldn't go without punishing him, either — it should have gone to a vote. I shrugged. That would have to wait. Confusing events were beginning to mount up, and I'm not a person well disposed to being confused. If events were unfolding, I needed to be with them and not behind them.

"I'll deal with you when I get back," I said, picking up my car keys and whistling for the Quarkbeast. "Keep an eye on the phones, and stay away from Lady Mawgon."

"Where are you going?"

"To find out what's going on."

"You're going to investigate ConStuff?"

"They're just after profit. To get to bottom of this, I need to speak to the real player — the dragon himself."

"Hmm," said Tiger. "It *sounds* like a good idea, but how in heck do you get to Maltcassion? Put a toe between the marker stones, and you're hot dust. And even if you do make it through, there's nothing to say he won't incinerate you for your impudence."

I smiled. "There's someone who can help me. A foundling like you and me. He is a fountain of encyclopedic knowledge that not only puts the reference section of the kingdom's central library in the shade, but also ensures he has won every pub quiz in the land."

"You mean—?"

"Right," I said. "William of Anorak."

TWELVE

William of Anorak

I stopped at the library to get some background information. William of Anorak was expensive and notoriously dull—even the hardiest soul could barely last twelve minutes in his company. The more I knew going in, the better. I read as much about dragons as I could, which wasn't much. No one had ever done a study, and apart from one blurred photograph of a dragon in flight taken in 1922, no one had any idea what one looked like. I thumbed through a book of zoology and discovered that they weren't a protected species; no one had even bothered to classify them at all. According to naturalists, the dragon belonged to the animal kingdom for sure, almost definitely to the vertebrates, and was as likely as not a reptile. Other than that—nothing.

But from my reading, I also learned one vital fact: according to the Dragonpact, there *had* to be a Last Dragonslayer. Only he or she could pass the marker stones unharmed. And, I reasoned, they had to be living close by. Armed with this intelligence, I headed to the one place William would almost certainly be hanging out: Hereford's main train station. I was in luck. He was on platform six, staring at the rolling stock.

William of Anorak was about fifty and dressed in a hooded cloak of a rough material, tied at the waist with baling twine. He was nearly bald and peered out at me through thick pebble spectacles. He wore sandals carved from old car tires and a duffle coat so worn and threadbare that only the buttons remained.

I hailed him, and he looked up, made a wan smile, and replied to my greeting with *"The Audio Chameleon changes sound to fit in with its surroundings. On a busy street it sounds like a road drill, but in the front room it makes a noise like a ticking clock.* Good day!"

"My name is Jennifer Strange," I said. "I have need of your services."

"William of Anorak," said William of Anorak, offering a grubby hand and adding quickly, *"The Magna*

Carta was signed in 1215 at the bottom, just below where it says 'any cat who thinks this a totally groovy idea, sign here.'" He turned back to a coal truck and started to scribble a number in a dirty notebook held open with an elastic band.

"I need to know where to find the Last Dragon-slayer," I asked, following him down the row of coal trucks.

"I was last asked that question twenty-three years, two months, and six hours ago. *The only fish that begins and ends with a K other than the killer shark is the king-sized portion of haddock.*"

"And what was your answer?"

"*The record number of pockets in a single pair of trousers is nine hundred and seventy-two. Only three had zippers, and the combined loose change was enough to buy a goat at 1766 prices.* Four hundred moolah, please."

"Four hundred?" I repeated incredulously. My only possession was my Volkswagen Beetle, and it was barely worth a tenth of what he was asking.

"Four hundred moolah," replied William of Anorak firmly, "in cash. *There are three types of shridloo: desert, de-siree, and dessert. The desert shridloo is remarkable for not liv-ing in a desert. The desiree shridloo is indistinguishable from a potato, and the dessert shridloo is the edible variety.*"

"Do you have to keep reeling off useless facts?"

"Unfortunately so," replied William of Anorak, adjusting his glasses. "I have over seven million facts in my head and if I don't repeat them to myself in order, I run the risk of forgetting them completely. *Milton wrote Samson Agonistes.* Would you like to hear it?"

"No, thanks," I said hurriedly. "Who said, 'Never commit anything to memory you can't look up'?"

"It was Albert Einstein and I see your point, yet I am as much a victim of my own powers as those who have the misfortune to stay in my company. You have been here over two minutes; that is better than most. *Most people prefer carpooling when other people do it, and the average number of pips in a tangerine is 5.368.*"

"I have no money," I implored, "not even a twenty-moolah bill. But to know the answer to my question, I will gladly give you everything I possess."

"Which is? *An anagram of moonlight is thin gloom, and the average troll can eat fifteen legs at one sitting.*"

"A 1958 Volkswagen Beetle with a registration that expires next week, a few books, and half a piano."

William of Anorak looked up and stopped scribbling in his pad. *"The most favorite boy's name is James; the least favorite is Gzxkls.* How can you have half a piano?"

"It's a long story, but basically I'm a musical duet pen pal with another foundling in San Mateo."

He continued to stare at me. *"A red setter is so stupid*

even the other dogs notice, and cats aren't really friendly; they're just cozying up to the dominant life form as a hedge against extinction. You're a foundling? From where?"

"The Lobsterhood."

A smile crossed his grubby, unshaven features. "You're *that* Jennifer Strange? The one at Kazam with the Quarkbeast?" I nodded and pointed at the Quarkbeast sitting in the car. He had once idly chewed his way through a locomotive's drive wheel and hadn't been allowed on railroad property since.

"*In the first photograph ever taken,*" said William, staring at me thoughtfully, "*someone blinked, and they had to begin again from scratch. It set the industry back two decades, and the problem has still not been properly rectified.* You were left in that Beetle when a foundling, yet you would give it to me?"

"I would."

"Then I will tell you the answer to your question for free. You will find Brian Spalding, worshipful Dragonslayer, appointed by the Mighty Shandar himself and holder of the sacred sword Exhorbitus—"

"Yes, yes?"

"Probably at the Dog and Ferret on Wimpole Street."

I thanked him profusely and shook his hand so hard, I could hear his teeth rattle.

"There's one other thing!" He beckoned me to lean

closer, then whispered, "*The largest deposit of natural mar-zipan ever discovered is a two-meter-thick seam lying beneath Cumbria.* Not a lot of people know that. Good luck, Miss Strange, and may you always walk in the shadow of the Lobster."

THIRTEEN

Brian Spalding

I thanked William of Anorak and hurried off toward the Dog and Ferret. It was closed due to King Snodd's strict licensing laws, which dictated that bars should be shut when you wanted a drink. So I sat down on a bench next to a very old man who had skin like a pickled walnut and eyes sunk deep in his head. He wore a neat blue suit and a Homburg hat, and he carried a cane with a silver top. He looked at me with great interest.

"Good afternoon, young lady," said the old man in a chirpy voice, tipping his head back to allow the warmth of the sun to fall upon his face.

"Good afternoon, sir," I replied, meeting politeness with politeness, as Mother Zenobia had taught me.

"Is that your Quarkbeast?" he asked, his eyes following the creature as it sniffed suspiciously at a statue of St. Grunk the Probably Fictitious.

"He's totally harmless," I replied. "All that stuff about Quarkbeasts eating babies is just fear-mongering by the papers."

"I know," he replied. "I used to have a Quarkbeast myself. Fiercely loyal creatures. Where did you find him?"

"I was at Starbucks," I replied, "about two years ago. The manager said to me, 'Your Quarkbeast is making the customers pass out in shock,' and I turned round and *Quark*, there he was, staring at me. So I said he wasn't mine, and they went to call the Beastcatcher, and I know what they do with Quarkbeasts, so I said he was mine after all and took him out. He's been with me ever since."

The old man nodded thoughtfully. "I rescued mine from a Quarkbaiting ring," he said, shuddering at the thought. "Frightfully cruel sport. He could chew his way through a London bus *lengthwise* in under eight seconds. A good friend. Does yours ever hum?"

"Hum?"

"Sort of like wind in telegraph wires."

"Not that I'm aware of. I'm not even sure if he's a boy or a girl. I wouldn't know how to tell, and quite frankly, it might be undignified to try to find out."

"They don't procreate in the usual manner," said the

old man. "They utilize quantum reproduction—they're just suddenly there, seemingly out of nothing."

I didn't know this and told him so.

"Quarkbeasts always arrive in pairs," added the old man knowledgeably. "Somewhere there will be an anti-Quarkbeast—a mirror image of your own. If paired Quarkbeasts come together, they disappear in a flash of energy. Remember the explosion last year in Hythe, which they claimed was a gas explosion?"

"Yes?" I said slowly, for the explosion had left a crater twelve meters deep in a housing estate, and fourteen dead.

"It was an unlucky confluence of Quarkbeasts. A separated pair came together quite by chance. They're lonely creatures—they have to be. Misunderstood too."

This was indeed true. I'd owned mine for six months before the lingering suspicion that I might be eaten alive gave way to genuine affection.

The old man paused to give a coin to a beggar lady collecting for the Troll War Widows Fund, then added, "Are you waiting for something?"

"I'm waiting for *someone*."

"Ah!" he replied. "Me, also." He sighed deeply and looked at his watch. "I wait for many years, but still Jennifer Strange does not appear."

"I'm sorry?" I said with a start. "Who did you say you were waiting for?"

"Jennifer Strange."

"But I'm Jennifer Strange!"

"Then," replied the old man with the ghost of a smile, "my wait is over!"

By the time I recovered from this shock, he had jumped to his feet and was walking swiftly along the pavement.

"Quickly, quickly," he muttered. "I wondered when you were going to turn up!"

"Who *are* you?" I asked, perplexed. "And how in the world did you know my name?"

"I," said the old man, stopping and turning so suddenly that I almost ran into him, "am Brian Spalding!"

"The Last Dragonslayer?"

"At your service."

"Then I must ask you——" I began, but the old man interrupted me again and crossed the road in front of a bus that had to swerve to avoid him.

"You've taken your time in getting here, young lady. I thought you would arrive when I was about sixty years of age, to give me a bit of a retirement, but no——look here." He stopped and showed me his face, which was wrinkled and soft like a prune.

"Look at me now! I am over a hundred and twelve!" He strode toward the opposite pavement and waved his cane angrily at a taxi that had to do an emergency stop just inches from his shins. "Confound you, sir!" he shouted at the cabbie. "Driving like a madman!"

"But how do you know my name?" I asked again, still confused.

"Simplicity itself," he replied. "The Mighty Shandar wrote a list of all the Dragonslayers that were to come, so the old Dragonslayer would know the new apprentices and not employ some twerp who would bring dishonor to the craft. You were chosen for your calling over four centuries ago, my girl, and rightly or wrongly, you will take your vows."

"But my name's not *actually* Jennifer Strange," I said. "I'm a foundling—I don't know what my name is!"

"It's Jennifer Strange enough for the Mighty Shandar," the old man said cheerily.

"I'm going to be a Dragonslayer?"

"Goodness me, no!" he chuckled. "You are to be an *apprentice* Dragonslayer."

"But I only started looking for you this morning—"

The old man stopped again and fixed me with his bright blue eyes. "Think of a huge feat of magic."

I thought of moving Hereford's cathedral two feet to the left, then nodded.

"Good. Then double it. Double it again, multiply by four, and then double *that*. The answer is one-tenth the size of the Old Magic involved here."

I leaned against a lamppost for support and tried to get my breath. This was all too confusing. I was half-expecting myself to be involved *somewhere* in all this — but not in the thick of it. I didn't do magic — I managed it.

"Wait," I said, as uncertainty and a mild panic suddenly washed over me. "I'm not sure I want to be a Dragonslayer's apprentice."

"Sometimes choice is a luxury that fate does not let us afford, Miss Strange. We're here." He was pointing across the road to a small house, one of many in a row of ordinary-looking terraced dwellings. The building had two large green garage doors, and painted on the road outside was a faded yellow hatched box with the words DRAGONSLAYER, NO PARKING in large letters. The old man opened the front door and beckoned me in.

He turned on the lights. "Behold!" he said. "The Dragonstation!"

The interior was large and airy and seemed to be living quarters and garage all rolled into one. At one side of the room was a kitchenette and living area with a large table, sofa, and TV; in the other half, parked in front of the double doors, was an old Rolls-Royce armored car. The car was of heavy riveted construction and had emergency lights like a police car. Two twin-tone sirens were bolted to the turret, and all over the vehicle were sharp copper spikes, protruding in every direction like a large metallic porcupine and reminding me of the armor that Dragon-slayers and their steeds had donned all those years ago.

"A Rolls!" I exclaimed.

"It is *never* a Rolls, young lady," admonished the old man. "Neither is it a Roller. The Slayermobile is a Rolls-Royce, and don't you forget it."

"Sorry."

"Times have moved on a bit, you know," he went on. "I started with a horse but changed to the Rolls-Royce when they demolished the stables to make way for the shopping center. I've never used it, although it remains in tiptop mechanical condition. This is the hot line." He pointed to a red telephone covered by a glass dome, much like those in bakeries that keep the cakes fresh.

"If it rings, it means there's a dragon attack going on somewhere. That's where we get the word *hotline*—dragons incinerating stuff."

"So that's where it comes from," I said. Then I added, "Has it ever rung?"

"Not once in four centuries for any dragon-related business, although we have recently been getting calls for Benny's Pizza—the numbers are quite similar. This way."

I followed the old man over to the far wall, upon which hung a lance with a sharp tip that glistened dangerously. On a table beneath it lay an exquisite sword with a long blade that ended in a large hilt, bound with leather and adorned with a ruby the size of an orange.

"Exhorbitus," said the old man in a soft, reverential voice. "The sword of a Dragonslayer. Only a Dragonslayer or his apprentice may touch it. One finger of an unauthorized hand, and *voof!*"

"*Voof?*"

"*Voof.*"

"Quark," said the Quarkbeast, who understood something important when he heard it.

"Someone tried to steal it once," continued the Dragonslayer. "Broke in at the back. Touched the ruby and was carbonized in less time than it takes to wink." I withdrew my hands quickly, and the old man smiled.

"Watch this," he said, picking up the sword with a deftness that belied his old age. He swished it about elegantly and then made a swipe in the direction of a chair. I thought he had missed, but he hadn't. He prodded the chair, and it fell into two pieces, neatly cleaved by the keen blade.

"As sharp as nothing else on earth. It will cut through carbide steel as though it were a wet paper bag."

"Why is it called Exhorbitus?"

"Probably because it was very expensive."

He replaced Exhorbitus on the desk while I looked around. All over the walls were lurid paintings of dragons and how they attacked, how they drank, how they fed, and the best way to sneak up on them. I pointed to a large oil painting of an armored Dragonslayer doing battle with a flame-breathing dragon. You could almost sense the heat and the danger, the sharpness of the talons and the clanking of armor.

"You?"

The old man laughed.

"Dear me, no! That painting is of Augustus of Delft doing battle with Janus during Mu'shad Waseed's failed dragon campaign. He was doing frightfully well right up until the moment when he was sliced into eight more or less equal parts." He turned to me more seriously. "I've been the Dragonslayer for ninety-one years, and I'm only the seventh since the Mighty Shandar finalized the Dragonpact. None of us has even set foot inside a Dragonland. But that's not to say we don't know a thing or two about dragons."

He tapped his head. "All the knowledge since the first Dragonslayer went to do battle is up here. Every plan, every attack, every outcome, every failure. All this information has been here ready and waiting just in case. *But it has never been needed!* Not one dragon has ever transgressed the Dragonpact. Not one single burned village, stolen cow, or eaten farmer. I'm sure you'll agree that the Mighty Shandar has done a pretty good job."

"But that's all changed."

His face fell. "Indeed. Events, I fear, are soon to be

realized. There is a prophecy in the air. It's like cordite and paraffin. Can you smell it?"

"I'm afraid not."

"Must be the drains, then. The pre-cogs say I am to kill the last dragon, and I will not falter in the face of my destiny. Shortly I am to do battle with Maltcassion, but I cannot do it alone. I need an apprentice. That person is *you*. Next Sunday at noon I'm to go and destroy him, and you must help me prepare."

"But there's no reason for you to go up there," I pointed out. "He has not transgressed the Dragonpact in any way."

The Dragonslayer shrugged. "There are still four days left; much can and will happen. This is bigger than me and bigger than you. Whether we like it or not, we will play our parts. Few of us understand the reason we are placed here; be grateful that you have so clear an objective."

I digested his words carefully. I still did not hold that the dragon had to die, or that premonitions are certain to come true. But it struck me that the Dragonslayer's apprentice might be well placed to ensure the dragon's survival. If I was to be anything other than a passive observer in the next few days, I was going to have to move fast.

"How do I become your apprentice?"

"I was beginning to think you'd never ask," he replied as he looked at the clock nervously. "It usually takes ten years of study, commitment, and deep learning, and the attainment of a spiritual oneness, but since we are in a bit of a hurry, I can give you the accelerated course."

"And how long does that take?"

"About a minute. Place your hand on this book."

He had taken a battered volume entitled *The Dragonslayer's Manual* from a small cupboard. I placed my hand on the worn leather and felt something like electricity tremble in my fingers, run up my arm, and tingle along my spine. As I closed my eyes, images of battle entered my head, memories of Dragonslayers long dead, passing on the wisdom of centuries to me. I could see the dragons in front of me, their faces, their ways, their habits; I felt the beat of a wing and heard the whoosh of fire as a dragon set fire to a village. I was upon a horse, galloping across a grassy plain, a dragon bellowing a fearful yell and igniting an oak tree, which burst into fire like a bomb.

Then I was in an underground cavern, listening to a dragon telling me stories of long ago, of a home far from here, a land with three moons and a violet sky. He spoke of a hope that humans and dragons could live together, of old things passing away and a new life without strife.

Then we were on the coast, running along the beach

with a dragon splashing beyond the surf line. I could see the images, and smell them and almost taste them . . . when abruptly, it all stopped.

"Time's up!" said the old man, grinning. "Did you get it all?"

"I'm not sure."

"Then answer me this: Who was the second Dragonslayer of the Kingdom of Hereford?"

"Octavius of Dewchurch," I said without thinking.

"And the name of the last horse in my service?"

"Tornado."

"Correct. You have the knowledge. Now swear on the name of the Mighty Shandar and the Old Magic that ties you to your calling that you will uphold every rule of the Dragonpact until you are less than dust."

"I swear."

There was a crackle of electricity, and a fierce wind blew inside the building. Overhead I heard a peal of thunder, and somewhere a horse whinnied. The Quarkbeast quarked loudly and ran under the table as a globe of ball lightning flew down the chimney, floated across the room, and evaporated with a bright flash and the pungent smell of ozone.

As the wind subsided, the old man became unsteady and sat on a nearby chair.

"Is anything the matter?" I asked him.

"I am sorry if I have deceived you, my child," he

murmured softly, the brisk energy of not more than two minutes ago having left him entirely.

"What do you mean?" I asked anxiously.

"I have been economical with the truth," he answered sadly. "Sometimes it is necessary for the greater good. You are not an apprentice. You are the Dragonslayer proper. I will not be joining you on Sunday. You will go alone."

"No!"

"I'm afraid so. You were late in arriving, my child; Old Magic kept me from the ravages of nature. I am not one hundred and twelve but almost one hundred and fifty — and I can feel the years advancing by the second. Good luck, my child, in whatever and however you do. Fear not for me because I fear not for myself. The keys to the Rolls-Royce are in that drawer over there. Check the oil and water daily, and" — here his voice started to falter — "you will find living accommodation up those stairs. The sheets are clean. I have prepared for your arrival every morning for thirty years." If his face had been wrinkled when I met him, it became twice as wrinkled as the years poured onto his ancient body.

"Wait!" I urged him. "You cannot go now! Who is to follow me?"

"No one, my child. Your name was the last on Shandar's list. Maltcassion will die in your tenure. You are the Last Dragonslayer."

"But I have so much to ask you!"

"You are a clever girl," he coughed, his voice growing weak. "You will do well on your own accord. Be true to yourself, and you will not fail. But please, do one thing for me."

"Anything."

He handed me a scrap of paper. "I gave my watch to be repaired last Tuesday. Would you fetch it and give it to the serving lady named Eliza at the Dog and Ferret, with my love?"

"Of course," I replied, my eyes growing misty as my new friend aged rapidly in front of me.

"And it is prepaid, the repair," he added. "So don't let the cheeky monkey charge you twice."

"I understand."

"One last thing," he murmured. "Will you fetch me a glass of water?"

I left him and went across to the sink. "I must just ask you," I said as I filled a glass, "about the link between magic and dragons. My mentor the Great Zambini was of the opinion that—"

I returned with the glass, then stopped. He must have wanted to spare my feelings, for there was nothing left of him but his suit, hat, and silver-topped cane lying empty in a heap on the floor among a fine smattering of gray powder. I'd never gained and lost a friend so quickly, and I hoped he would have thought of me as a friend too.

Thus it was that I, Jennifer Strange, sixteen years next month and loyal subject of King Snodd IV in the Kingdom of Hereford, took on the rights and responsibilities of the Last Dragonslayer. It wasn't what I expected, but then I don't know *what* I had been expecting. That's the thing about destiny: It can't be predicted, and it's usually pretty odd.

"Quark," said the Quarkbeast.

"Shh," I said, sitting on the sofa, my mind in a whirl. "I'm thinking."

FOURTEEN

The Dragonlands

I called Tiger.

"It's Jenny," I told him. "Is everything all right?"

"Everyone's glaring at me and mumbling in low tones."

"You're going to have to deal with that for a while."

"How did you get on with finding out about dragons?"

"Quite well, actually," I replied slowly. "I think I'm the Last Dragonslayer."

There was silence.

"I said I think—"

"I heard what you said. I just don't think it's very

funny. I put my neck on the block as a kind of foundling solidarity thing, and you don't take any of it seriously."

"I'm not kidding. I'm the Last Dragonslayer. I'm at the Dragonstation now and have the sword and everything."

There was another pause.

"This kind of changes things," said Tiger. "You'll be famous and asked what you're going to do and who you're going out with and what food you eat and what your opinion is and whether you'll endorse junky products and stuff."

"I'm not looking forward to it, nor to the possibility of killing a dragon. But at least I get to actually find something out about Maltcassion—and with the sword Exhorbitus, I'll finally be able to trim the Quarkbeast's claws."

"That would be helpful," admitted Tiger. "All that *click-click-click* on the floor is a bit annoying." He paused again. "Does this mean I have to run Kazam?"

I told him that I was sure I could do both, and that I would try to smooth things over with Lady Mawgon and Moobin and the others. This seemed to satisfy him, and after telling him to go and hide in a wardrobe if things got bad, I told him I would be home as soon as I had sorted a few things out.

I replaced the phone slowly. I walked around the

apartment a few times, touched Exhorbitus, and was relieved to find I didn't go *voof,* then had a look around in the Slayermobile, which smelled of leather and warm oil. I called Mother Zenobia, who couldn't be disturbed because she was taking her nap, then drank a cup of tea while I walked nervously around the room some more, fervently wishing Mr. Zambini were here. *He* would know what to do.

"Quark," said the Quarkbeast, pointing a claw at a painting of the Dragonlands.

"You're right," I said, taking a deep breath. I wasn't going to learn anything sitting around in the Dragonstation drinking tea, so I mounted the lance on the side of the Rolls-Royce and clipped Exhorbitus onto the bracket next to the riveted iron door. The doors to the garage opened easily on well-oiled hinges, and the Rolls-Royce whispered into life. I paused for breath, and then, with the Quarkbeast riding shotgun, I edged the Slayermobile out into traffic.

It was busy on the streets, yet the traffic peeled out of my way. Although no one had seen the Slayermobile before, most could guess what it was, especially as it had DRAGONSLAYER ON CALL written on the side in big letters. It was tricky to drive, the steering was heavy, and I misjudged a corner once and hit a bollard, but the sharp spikes on the Rolls-Royce simply sliced through the iron as if it were butter. Children pointed, grownups stared, and even drunks saluted me with their half-nibbled blocks of industrial-grade marzipan. Cars stopped at lights to let me cross unhindered, and several times a confused policeman, thinking I must be a new secret weapon of King Snodd's or something, halted traffic and waved me through a red light, saluting as I passed.

I reached the Dragonlands in under forty minutes and drove carefully through the campers and tents that had increased dramatically since the previous night. Word had gotten around, and people were traveling to the Kingdom of Hereford from all over the Ununited Kingdoms. Several catering vans had turned up, eager to turn a profit wherever crowds gathered. The mass of people waved excitedly as I drove by, running for their balls of string and claiming stakes in case this was the end of the dragon. They would have to be disappointed.

I took a deep breath and drove between the marker stones. There was a crackle and a rumble. If I had tried the same thing an hour ago, I would have been vaporized. I parked the Rolls-Royce and waved cheerfully to the crowd on the other side of the marker stones; the crowd gaped back like fish.

"New Dragonslayer!" I shouted by way of explanation. "Just going to go and do . . . my . . . thing."

When I turned around, I jumped—for in front of me, here in the Dragonlands, was a man. He was quite unlike any man I had ever seen before. He was tall and graceful, with a shock of white hair, a craggy complexion, and gleaming eyes that sparkled and danced. Dressed in a black suit and cape, he wore a large amethyst ring on his finger and carried a staff of willow. I knew instantly who he was.

"The Mighty Shandar!" I gasped, and dropped to my knees.

"Quark, *quark*," said the Quarkbeast, and explosively shed several steel-tipped scales in his excitement, one of which embedded itself into a nearby tree with a *twong*.

"You must be a Dragonslayer or an apprentice," said a warm voice that sounded like how I hoped my father would speak, "for only they may pass the marker stones."

"I am, sir," I muttered, unsure of how to address the most powerful wizard the world had ever known.

"I expect you have many questions," continued the Mighty Shandar.

"Well, yes, I do," I replied, looking up, "in particular, how the whole dragon/magic deal—"

"Questions that I cannot hope to answer."

I got to my feet. "How's that?" I asked, but the wizard ignored me.

"This is a recording, by the way," answered Shandar. Now that I looked closer, he seemed almost translucent, like a specter. The image flicked and rocked as he spoke, and I was surprised to find that a sorcery recording is not a lot better than a poor video recording. I waved a hand in front of his eyes, but he didn't react.

The Mighty Shandar continued, "You are the first Dragonslayer to venture onto the lands, and you are here for one of two reasons: one, you are curious, or two, the dragon violated the Dragonpact. If the reason is the former, then look and see and leave as soon as you can. If the reason is the latter, then look very carefully at the evidence of the suspected crime. There is much deceit in this world, and if there is even the slightest doubt in your mind, let the dragon live. One more point. Dragons can be deceitful, too. They often have a separate agenda and will manipulate the weak-minded for their own purposes. I wish you the best of luck. If you want to hear the message again, clap your hands once. If you want to delete this message, clap your hands twice. If you want to save this message then, oh, never mind."

He smiled as the image flicked twice and then faded from view, leaving me to mull over his words. Shandar's support of the dragons seemed unequivocal, yet it didn't seem as though he thought you could trust them. Confused, and with his warnings filling me with unease, I began my walk into the Dragonlands, the Quarkbeast at my heels.

The hill was mostly scrubby moorland of heather and bracken, full of wildlife that had learned to live without fear of man. Rabbits sniffed at my ankles, and feral cows and sheep paid me little or no heed as I walked past in the warm summer air. After an hour's climb across the empty moorland, I came across a small lake. I walked around the water's edge, peering at the fish in the clear waters and realizing what a loss this vast natural wildlife park would be if Maltcassion were gone. I reached the far side of the lake, walked through a spinney of silver birches, and then climbed a hill from where I could see deep into the Dragonlands. It was a landscape without power lines, buildings, or telephone poles. There were no roads, no trains, and no people. The vegetation had grown unchecked for centuries, and large oaks were interspersed among beech and elder.

I forded a river, stopped for a drink, and then followed the water into a forest of Douglas fir. As I did so, I noticed an eerie silence fall upon the land. The soft and lush undergrowth absorbed sound, so even my boots splashing through the brook seemed to make very little noise. After a few hundred yards, I noticed that old animal bones were scattered in the stream, so I guessed I was nearing my quarry. A little farther on I found several Spanish gold doubloons and a ruby the size of a man's fist lying in the bed of the stream. Within a few hundred yards more, I came across a large clearing in the forest.

"Quark," said the Quarkbeast as we stood on the smooth earth. In the center of the clearing was a large stone, not unlike the boundary stones that ringed the Dragonlands. There was an audible hum in the still air, and above us a light wind moved the upper branches of the trees. Hidden in the compacted earth were glimpses of gold and the flash of a jewel. Here indeed was the lair of a dragon. His food, his gold, his jewels. Everything, in fact, except a dragon. There was no cave of any sort. Other than a pile of rubble on one side of the clearing, there was nothing here at all. I turned to go when suddenly, in a clear and patient voice, came the words:

"Well, look what we have here: a *Dragonslayer!*"

FIFTEEN

Maltcassion

W ho's there?" I asked, my voice trembling. I looked around but could see no one. I was about to climb the odd pile of stones to get a better look around when I noticed, lying in the rubble, a fine red jewel about the size of a tennis ball. A leathery lid slid over the jewel and flipped back up again. I froze. The jewel moved as it looked me up and down, and Maltcassion spoke again.

"Bit young for a Dragonslayer, aren't you?"

The pile of rubble moved, and I felt the ground shiver. He unwrapped his tail and stretched it out, then used it as a back scratcher just above where two wings were folded tightly against his spine.

"I'm sixteen," I muttered indignantly.

"Sixteen?"

"In two weeks. Actually, since I don't know precisely *when* I was born, I might already be sixteen. I may have been two weeks old when I was abandoned, but birthdays are always taken from the date you were left at the convent as a foundling, so—"

"You're babbling, whoever you are."

"I am, aren't I? Sorry. I'm not well acquainted with dragons."

"Few are," Maltcassion said with a soft chuckle. "Are you here to slay me?"

"No."

He raised his massive head from between his two front claws and looked at me curiously. Then he opened his mouth wide and yawned. Two large rows of teeth about the size of milk bottles presented themselves to me. The teeth were old and brown, and several had broken off. My eyes watered at the smell of his breath, a powerful concoction of rotting animal, vegetation, fish, and methane gas. He raised his head and coughed a large ball of fire into the air before looking at me again.

"Excuse me," he muttered apologetically, "the body grows old. Is that a Quarkbeast?"

"Yes."

Maltcassion moved closer to the Quarkbeast and studied him at length.

"Does he change color?"

"Only when there's too much silicon in his diet."

"Ah." The dragon dug his two front claws into the soil and pushed up with his hind legs to stretch, his claws moving through the hard-packed earth like twin plowshares. There was a loud *crack* from his back and he relaxed.

"Ooh!" he muttered. "That's better." His wings snapped open like a spring-loaded umbrella, and he beat them furiously, setting up a dust storm that made me cough. One wing was badly tattered; the membrane covering was ripped in several places. After a minute or two, he folded his wings delicately, then turned his attention back to me. He came closer and sniffed at me. Oddly, I felt no fear. Perhaps that was my Dragonslayer training; I didn't suppose I would have dared stand next to forty tons of fire-breathing dragon twenty-four hours ago without feeling at least some anxiety. A sharp rush of air tugged violently at me as he inhaled. He seemed satisfied at last and put his head down again, his scaly skin once more looking like nothing more than a huge pile of rubble.

"So, Dragonslayer," he asked loftily, "you have a name?"

"My name is Jennifer Strange," I announced as grandly as I could, "with two N's."

"In 'Strange' or 'Jennifer'?"

"Jennifer."

"Oh," said the dragon. "Just checking."

"I present myself to you by way of introduction," I continued. "I sincerely hope that I have no need of my calling, and that you and the citizenry —"

"Claptrap," said Maltcassion, "pure claptrap. But I thank you anyway. Before you go, could you do me a favor?"

"Certainly."

He rolled onto his side and lifted a front leg, pointing with the other to an area just behind his shoulder blade. "Old wound. Would you mind?"

I clambered onto his chest and looked at the area he indicated. Just behind a leathery scale was a rusty object protruding from a wound that had obviously been trying to heal for a while. I grasped the object with both hands and, pressing my feet against his rough hide, pulled with all my might. I was beginning to think that it would never come out when I was suddenly on my back in the dust. In my hands was a very rusted and very bent sword, which I threw aside.

"Thank you!" said Maltcassion, reaching to lick the wound with a tongue the size of a mattress. "That's been annoying me for about four centuries. You may help yourself to some gold or jewels by way of payment, Miss Strange."

"I require no payment, sir."

"Really? I thought all mankind gravitated toward

things that are shiny. I'm not saying that's *necessarily* a bad thing, but when it comes to species development, it could be limiting."

"I'm not here for money. I'm here to do the right thing."

"Principled as well as fearless!" murmured Maltcassion with a chuckle. "*Quite* a Dragonslayer! You have a good heart. We were right to wait for you. You may leave now."

"*Wait* for me?" I asked. "What do you mean?" But he had finished speaking. He closed his jewellike eyes and shuffled to get more comfortable. I just stared at this huge untidy heap, the rarest animal on the entire planet. Here was a creature of extraordinary nobility and intelligence, and everyone actually *wanted* him to die so they could grab some land.

"It's a PR thing," said the dragon, half to itself.

"Sorry?"

"It's a public relations thing," he said again, opening his eyes and staring at me. "Why do people spend millions trying to save dolphins, yet eat tuna by the bucketful? Isn't that what you were thinking of?"

"You can read my thoughts?"

"Only when someone feels passionately about something. Ordinary thoughts are pretty dull. Powerful ideas have a life of their own; they carry on, unshakable, from person to person. Wouldn't you agree?"

He didn't wait for an answer but carried on. "Elephants, gorillas, buzonjis, dolphins, snow leopards, shridloos, tigers, lions, cheetahs, whales, seals, manatees, orangutans, pandas—what have all these got in common?"

"They're all endangered."

"Apart from that."

"They're all pretty big?" I hazarded.

"They're all *mammals,*" said Maltcassion contemptuously. "You seem to be making this planet into an exclusive mammals-only club. If seal cubs were as ugly as the average reptile, I wonder if you'd bother with them at all. But those big eyes and the cute barking and the soft fur, well, it just melts your little mammalian heart, doesn't it?"

"There are nonmammals that are protected," I argued, but Maltcassion wasn't impressed.

"Window dressing, nothing more. No one much cares about the reptiles, bugs, or fishes, unless, of course, they look nice. Seems a pretty crummy method of selecting species for survival, don't you think? If you want to redress your overtly mammal-supremacist attitudes, I should ban the words *cuddly, cute,* and *fluffy,* for a start."

I couldn't think of much to say, so I asked instead, "Can I come and see you again?"

"Why?"

"To ask you some questions."

"Why?"

"So we might know more about dragons."

"Humans," he scoffed. "Always so *inquiring* about stuff. Never satisfied with the status quo. It will be your downfall, but oddly enough, it's also one of your more endearing features."

"Do we have any others?"

"Oh yes, plenty."

"Such as?"

"Well, counting in base ten is pretty wild, for a start," he said, after giving the subject a moment's thought. "Base twelve is *far* superior. You also have extraordinary technical abilities, a terrific sense of humor, thumbs, being built inside-out—"

"Wait! Being built inside-out?"

"Of course. As far as the average lobster is concerned, mammals—with the possible exception of the armadillo—are built inside out. Any crab worth his claws will tell you the soft stuff should *definitely* be on the inside. Bones in the middle? Whoever designed you was having a serious off-day. Put it this way: If you lost a limb, would it grow back?"

"No."

"Me neither, but if we were a member of the crustacean family, we could expect a new limb the following year. Mind you, if we're talking about regeneration, we could go a step further and take a leaf out of the sponge book. There are sponges you can chop to pieces, whiz up in the blender, and then press through a sieve, and they'll *still* regenerate."

"Useful, maybe," I replied, "but I think there is a limit to the amount of fun you could have as a sponge."

"I think you have something there," conceded the dragon.

"You seem to know a lot about animals," I said.

"I'm always surprised that you all don't take more interest in other creatures. It's like living on a street and not knowing your next-door neighbor. If I were human, I'd start investing in a little kindness. When the arthropods rule the planet, all those lobster dishes and crab sticks could well be a cause of some regret."

"I don't think mammals are on the way out, Maltcassion."

"That's what the giant reptiles said. What are they now? Birds."

"So what are you saying?"

"Well, Darwin got it very nearly completely right. A remarkable brain for a human. But he overlooked one thing. Natural selection is also governed by a sense of humor. You would see it yourself if only your life span were long enough. Over ninety million years ago there was a small, brightly colored beetle named a sklhrrg beetle. It was beautiful. I mean *really* beautiful. Even the most brainless toad would stop and gaze adoringly. It strutted around the forest, preening and primping, being admired by all. A few thousand years of this, and it evolved into one of the most vain and obnoxious creatures you could possibly meet. It was all 'me, me, me.' Other beetles avoided it, and party invitations simply dried up. But nature adores a joke. Thirty million years later and what has it evolved into now?"

"I don't know."

"The dung beetle. Dull-colored and innocuous, it pushes dung around. Lives in it, eats it, lays its eggs in it. Don't tell me nature doesn't have a sense of humor!" Maltcassion grunted out a short burst of fire that I took to be a laugh, then muttered something about chameleons telling jokes in colors before he settled down, shut his eyes, and started to snore.

Since he didn't actually say I shouldn't return, I supposed he wouldn't mind if I came back. I stared at the heap of rubble, delighted at my good fortune so far. His tattered wing led me to assume that he couldn't fly, so I couldn't see him actually getting out to break the Dragonpact. I waited until I was sure he was actually asleep, then crept from the clearing and retraced my steps back toward the marker stones and the Rolls-Royce.

As I walked over the last rise, I saw that the crowd outside the Dragonlands had grown to include the press and TV stations; the Last Dragonslayer was news indeed. I walked down to the marker stones and stepped through the force field.

"Auster Old-Spott of the *Daily Winkle*," said one man in a shabby suit. "Can I ask your name?" He pushed a microphone in my face as another equally shabby newsman said, "Paul Tamworth of the *Clam*. Have you seen Maltcassion?"

"When do you expect to kill the dragon?" asked a third.

"How did you get to be a Dragonslayer?" asked another.

A man thrust his way through the crowd and showed me a contract. "My name is Oscar Pooch," he announced. "I represent Yummy Flakes breakfast cereals, and I'd like you to endorse our product. Ten thousand moolah a year. Do we agree? Sign here, please."

"Don't listen to him!" said another man, in a pinstriped suit. "Our company will offer you *twenty* thousand moolah for exclusive rights to represent Fizzi-Pop soft drinks. Sign here —"

"Wait!" I shouted.

The crowd went silent. All one hundred, two hundred; I don't know how many there were, but there were a lot. The cameramen from the TV stations trained their cameras on me, waiting for whatever I had to say. I took a deep breath and swallowed down my nervousness.

"My name is Jennifer Strange," I began, to the sound

of frantic scribbling from the newspapermen's notepads. "I am the new Dragonslayer. Charged by the Mighty Shandar himself, I will uphold the rules of the Dragonpact and protect the people from the dragon, and the dragon from the people. I will issue a full statement in due course. That is all."

I was impressed by the speech, but then I'd been bound to pick up a thing or two during Brian Spalding's one-minute accelerated Dragonslaying course. I retrieved the Rolls-Royce and headed back into town, the crush of journalists and photographers following me as best as they could. Brian Spalding had not alerted me to this sort of media attention, although twenty thousand moolah just to endorse Fizzi-Pop sounded like some very easy money indeed.

Gordon van Gordon

I returned to the Dragonstation to find the street crowded with even more journalists, TV crews, and on-lookers. The police had thoughtfully closed the road and erected barriers to keep the public on the far side of the street. I parked outside and jumped out of the Slayermobile to the rattle of cameras and popping of flashbulbs. I ignored them, more concerned with a small man dressed in a brown suit and matching derby hat on the front steps. He was aged about forty and tipped his hat respectfully as I placed the key in the lock. I wondered why he wasn't behind the barriers with the rest, and I soon found out.

"Miss Strange?" inquired the small man. "I've come about the job."

"Job?" I asked. "What job?"

"Why, the job as apprentice Dragonslayer, of course." He waved a copy of the *Hereford Daily Eyestrain* at me. "In the Situations Vacant page. 'Wanted—'"

"Let me see."

I took the paper, and sure enough, there it was in black and white: *Wanted, Dragonslayer's apprentice. Must be discreet, valiant, and trustworthy. Apply in person at 12 Slayer's Way.*

"I don't need an assistant," I told him.

"Everyone needs an assistant," said the small man in a jovial tone. "A Dragonslayer more than anyone. To deal with the fan mail, if nothing else."

I looked past the small man to perhaps thirty other people who had also replied to the ad. They all smiled cheerily and waved a copy of the paper at me. The small man raised an eyebrow quizzically.

"You're hired," I snapped. "First job, get rid of this bunch." I jerked my head in the direction of the wannabe apprentices and went inside. I shut the door and wondered what to do next.

On an impulse, I called Mother Zenobia. She seemed even more pleased to hear from me than usual.

"Jennifer darling!" she gushed. "I've just heard the news, and we are *so* proud! Just think, a daughter of the Great Lobster becoming a Dragonslayer!"

I was slightly suspicious. "How did you hear, Mother?"

"We've had some charming people around here asking all kinds of questions about you!"

"You didn't tell them anything, did you?" I had no desire to have my childhood splashed all over the tabloids. The pause at the other end of the phone answered my question.

"Was that wrong?" asked Mother Zenobia at length. I sighed. Mother Zenobia had taken over the role of a real mother almost perfectly, even that unique motherly quality of being able to acutely embarrass her child.

"It doesn't matter," I replied with a trace of annoyance in my voice.

"Jolly good!" she said brightly. "I've already accepted on your behalf an invitation to talk on *The Yogi Baird Daytime TV Show.*"

"Why would you do something like that?"

"They agreed to take on four foundlings as juniors in their office."

"Well, in that case, okay."

"*Excellent.* And if I may say so, I think Fizzi-Pop is a fine product. I've met a jolly pleasant young man who is very keen to talk to you."

I thanked her and hung up. The doors to the garage opened, and the small man in the brown suit expertly reversed in the Rolls-Royce. He hopped down from the armored car, put the sword and lance away—he could do so without being vaporized, since I had employed him—and offered me a small hand to shake.

"Gordon's the name," he said brightly, pumping my arm vigorously. "Gordon van Gordon Gordonson ap Gordon-Gordon of Gordon."

"I'll stick to 'Gordon,'" I said.

"It may save some time."

"Jennifer Strange," I announced. "Pleased to meet you."

"And you." He didn't stop shaking my hand. He seemed so happy to be here that he wanted everything to last as long as possible so he could savor it to the full.

"I don't know who put the ad in the paper, but it wasn't me," I told him.

"That's easily explained," he said with a grin. "It was me!"

"You? Why?"

"I wanted to be the first in line. Dragonslayers always need an assistant, so I thought I would save you the trouble of advertising."

"Very enterprising," I said slowly.

He raised his hat again. "Thank you. A Dragonslayer's apprentice has to be discreet, valiant, trustworthy, *and* enterprising."

"Gordon?"

"Yes?"

"Can I have my hand back?"

He apologized and let go. "So," he said. "What's our first move, chief?"

"Nothing yet. It might help to have some food in the house. The Quarkbeast likes to sleep in a trash can; you'll have to buy one from the hardware store, but make sure it's painted and not galvanized so he won't chew it. He eats dog food but isn't particular about the brand. He needs a link of heavy anchor chain to gnaw on each week and a spoonful of fish oil in his water dish every day — it keeps his scales shiny. Do you cook?"

"Yes."

"Well, I'm vegetarian but not particularly militant — you can eat what you want."

He had been scribbling down notes on his shirt cuff. I swore him to secrecy and told him about the prophecy of next Sunday. This filled him with greater enthusiasm than cooking, trash cans, or the Quarkbeast's peculiar eating habits.

"Great! I'll change the oil in the Slayermobile so when you come to do some slaying, we'll be ready, and—"

"Wait a minute!" I grabbed his lapel between my finger and thumb as he tried to hurry off. "I want to make this *very* clear. I don't ever intend to actually kill a dragon."

"So why are you a Dragonslayer?" Gordon asked with blinding directness.

"Because . . . because . . . well, that's the way Old Magic made it happen."

"Old Magic?" he said uneasily. "Wait a minute. You never mentioned anything about Old Magic in the advertisement."

"Didn't I?"

"No. We're going to have to discuss new terms if Old Magic is involved."

I thought for second. "Hang on. Gordon, *you* wrote the advertisement!"

He paused. "I did, didn't I?" he said at length. "Well, I better let it go this once then." He looked crestfallen but soon perked up when I told him that, like it or not, I would need a press officer, so he dashed off to get some paper and crayons to write a quick press release.

By now it was early evening, and I needed to get back to Zambini Towers. But I wasn't more than ten paces out the door before a scrum of people ran toward me. The first to talk to me was a businessman wearing a very large hat and an expensive suit.

"Jethro Ballscombe," he said, passing me a business card the size of roofing slate. "I want to make *you* a very rich young woman." He grinned at me, showing a ridiculously large gold tooth that must make metal detectors in airports throw an electronic fit. He thought my silence indicated assent rather than a curious interest in his dentition, so he continued, "Do you know how much people will pay to come and see a real live dragon?" He grinned wildly, as though expecting me to leap up and down or something.

"You want to put Maltcassion in a zoo?"

He put an arm around my shoulder and hugged me as though I were his long-lost niece.

"Not so much a zoo as his own special one-species family entertainment exclusive themed adventure park." He waved a hand in the air and stared into the middle distance to make his point.

"DragonWorld™," he gasped, as if he hardly dared to say the word due to the size and breathtaking audacity of the project. "You and me, partners, fifty-fifty. What do you say?" He smirked at me expectantly, moolah signs in his eyes, waiting for my reply.

"I'll mention it to him," I said coldly. "But he'll probably say no."

"Mention it to who?" the man asked, genuinely confused.

"Why, Maltcassion, of course!"

He slapped me on the back and laughed so loudly I thought he would surely choke.

"I like a girl with a sense of humor! Well, that's

agreed then. You won't regret it!" He shook my hand heartily and bade me goodbye, climbed into a waiting limousine, and was gone.

Another man tried to collar me about licensing a range of collectible ornamental plates entitled the World of the Dragonslayer, and there was even another offer from Fizzi-Pop, this time for forty thousand moolah. I told them I wasn't interested and then, with the press clamoring for a further statement, slipped back inside. I found Gordon van Gordon vacuuming up the gray ash that had once been Brian Spalding.

"I know, I know," he said at my look of shock. "I'm going to put him in this empty syrup tin. You can take him up to the Dragonlands next time you go."

"Fair enough." I looked for a back door and opened it onto an alleyway that was, thankfully, empty. I made my way quickly to the Dog and Ferret, where I had left my Volkswagen, and drove from there back to Zambini Towers.

SEVENTEEN

The Truth about Mr. Zambini

"H ello," I said to Tiger as I walked into the Kazam offices. "How are things?"

"These are for you," he said, handing me a stack of messages that didn't relate to Kazam at all, but to me.

"The *Mollusc on Sunday* wants to do a feature on me," I said, flicking through the messages, "and this one's an offer of marriage."

"There are another five of those. Did you see Lady Mawgon on your way in?"

I looked up. "No."

"She's been looking at me in a funny way. I think she's scheming."

"She's *always* scheming," I replied, dropping the

messages into the trash. "I'm not sure she can even look at an apple cart without wanting to overturn it."

I walked across to the Quarkbeast's snack cupboard and tossed him a tin of sardines, which he crunched up gratefully. I spent the next hour explaining to Tiger what had happened that day: Brian Spalding, the accelerated dragonslaying course, the Dragonlands, Maltcassion, and talking to the press on the way out.

"I was going to bring Exhorbitus to show you," I concluded, "but I didn't want to arouse any suspicion."

"I think it's a bit late for that. Have you seen the TV recently?"

He switched on the set. UKBC was now revealing the drama unfolding on our doorstep with almost constant coverage. The screen was of Sophie Trotter again, this time up by the marker stones.

"There are an estimated five hundred thousand people gathered around the Dragonlands," she said, looking behind her at the chaotic scrum. "There have been reports of jostling that sent one man through the boundary, where he was vaporized in a bright blue flash. The police are worried that there might be a bigger disaster, so are attempting to move the crowds back from the marker stones." There was a bright flash behind her. "Whoops, there goes another one. I must see if we can ask a grieving relative how they feel."

I switched off the television and looked at my watch. "It's time for you to go home."

"I am home."

"Me, too," I replied. "I mean it's time to stop work."

"I knew what you meant," returned Tiger. "It's just that even with everyone in the building except you hating me —"

"Quark."

"Sorry, everyone except you and the Quarkbeast hating me, I just wanted you to know that I've never been happier. But can I ask you something?"

"Sure."

"What *did* happen to Mr. Zambini?"

I looked across at him. If I couldn't trust him now, I couldn't trust him ever.

"Okay, here it is, but you must promise not to tell any of the others. You should know that the Great Zambini was once one of the best. I use his redundant accolade out of respect. When he was young and powerful, he held the magician's world teleport record of eighty-five miles, although unofficially he had managed well over a hundred. He could conjure up showers of fish and manipulate matter to a level that would make Moobin's lead-into-gold escapade seem like kitchen chemistry. He paid for the Towers personally and gathered together the sorcerers within to try and keep the *spirit* of the Mystical Arts alive, even when he knew that wizidrical powers were fading. He gave everything he had to Kazam. He would work every hour of the day and night, and I with him. He was like a father to me. Kind, generous, hard-working, and utterly committed not just to his calling but to protecting and supporting those within it."

"It sounds like he was an honorable man."

"He was. But *still* money was short, and he was forced to do the one thing that sorcerers should never do. An act of such gross betrayal to his art that if it were made common knowledge, his reputation would be destroyed forever, and he would die a broken man, humiliated and shunned by his peers."

"You mean—?"

"Right. He did children's parties."

Tiger put his hand over his mouth. "He lowered himself, for *them?* For Lady Mawgon and Moobin and those batty sisters whose name I can't remember?"

"All of them. It was the only way to keep Kazam going. He used to do the events out of town, of course, and in disguise. Simple stuff: rabbits out of hats, card tricks, minor levitation. But one afternoon he must have had a surge. He vanished in a puff of green smoke during his finale. Hasn't come back."

"So when you said he'd disappeared, you really meant it."

"Totally. But I've not given up hope. He spontaneously rematerializes every now and then, and although Kevin Zipp can give me a time or a place for a reappearance, he can't give me both — it's easy to be in the right place, but a week late — or at the right time, but in the wrong village. There's a lot of countryside out there."

"And a lot of Now."

"Tons. And I can't get the others to help because I'd have to reveal what he'd been up to, and I can't see the old man humiliated. On the plus side, the kids thought he was great, and a standing ovation from five-year-olds is not to be sniffed at."

"But that's not the whole story, is it?" said Tiger, holding up a battered copy of *Simpkin's Foundling Law*.

"No," I replied. "Until he comes back or is declared dead or lost, he can't sign us out of our indentured servitude. Technically speaking, we're here until we die."

Tiger closed the book. "That's what I thought."

"He'll come back," I assured him, "or failing that, I'll confess everything, and we'll have him declared lost and have our servitude assigned to his successor. In any event, I've still got two years to run, and you've got six. Lots can happen." I smiled at him, and he smiled back. It was my way of telling him not to worry, and his way of agreeing that he shouldn't.

"I'm going to go and see Moobin," I told him. "I need to know how the wizards are doing. Keep well away from Lady Mawgon, and I'll see you later."

Big Magic

I found Wizard Moobin in his room. He had repaired the door but was still busy tidying up after the explosion. There was almost nothing unbroken. The power of magic can be devastating when uncontrolled, and ever since the Blix episode, individual practitioners were required to keep incantations below the half-megashandar level. Blix had made use of a loophole to store wizidrical power and use it on a spree of subjugation. The six-gigashandar blast that had heralded the end of Blix's brief reign had taken out not just him but two kingdoms and an estimated half million people.

There was someone else in Moobin's room, too, someone I didn't recognize.

"Ah," said Moobin when he saw me, "it's you. This is Mr. Stamford, a lapsed sorcerer from Mercia. He'll be staying with me for a few days. Mr. Stamford, this is Jennifer Strange."

Stamford was a sallow man with greasy hair. He peered at me cautiously and shook my hand.

"You're here because of the Dragondeath?" I asked.

"I think so," he replied after a moment's thought. "You know that feeling when you go into a room and then can't remember what you're there for?"

"Yes."

"It's *exactly* like that. I don't know why I'm here, I just feel that I should be." And he fell silent.

"He's the third to arrive since this morning," said Wizard Moobin. He stared at me for a moment. "Tiger Prawns was out of order going public and sabotaging the ConStuff deal, you know."

"I know. He was doing it to stop me from resigning."

"It was noble, I grant you that. And most of us respect honor, sacrifice, nobility, and ethical stances. Sadly, Lady Mawgon doesn't. She wanted to have you both replaced and asked Mother Zenobia to send a shortlist of new foundlings so we could start interviewing."

"That's not how it works."

"It's how Lady Mawgon works."

"What happened?"

"Mother Zenobia told her they'd run out."

I smiled. Mother Zenobia had hundreds of foundlings ready to take up servitude. That must have made Mawgon even angrier.

"So what's she doing now?"

"Lady Mawgon? Marching around the corridors, gnashing her teeth, and seething, I imagine. But that's not the biggest issue right now, is it?"

"You saw the news on TV?"

"It was hard to miss it. It surprised us all, I must say. How did you get to be the Last Dragonslayer?"

I told him briefly how it all came about, and he nodded sagely. I added that it wouldn't alter my commitment to Kazam, but that I might be busy on Sunday, about noon.

"We all wish you the best, of course," he said, then added, "except Lady Mawgon, perhaps, who would probably be delighted to see you eaten. I would ignore her."

"I plan to."

Moobin thought for a moment. "You're no longer a bystander, Jennifer. You're a player. And not just in the world of Dragonslaying — but magic."

"I figured that," I said slowly. "Perhaps this is a good time to tell me what Big Magic is, and where you get it?"

Mr. Stamford and Moobin exchanged glances and nodded to each other.

"There was a time before magic," said Mr. Stamford, "and there will be a time when magic has gone. In between those times, the power of magic will ebb and flow like the tide. But unlike the tide, it is entirely possible that the power of magic, aided by the destructive agencies of distrust, denial, and disuse, will recede forever and *never* return."

"That's unthinkable."

"We are all agreed on *that* score," said Moobin, "but the news isn't all bad. There is always an opportunity to rekindle that spark and bring the tide of power back into flood—and the flood brings on renewal. Renewal of the power of magic."

"And that opportunity is Big Magic?" I asked.

"A chance to recharge the batteries, so to speak," continued Wizard Moobin. "But at times of low power, sorcerers are less likely to see the signs of a Big Magic. We never know when it will be, or what form it will take. The last time Big Magic took place was two hundred and thirty years ago, with the appearance of the star Aleutius in the evening sky. If Brother Thassos of Crete had not seen it as the sign it was, magic might have vanished for good."

"But where does magic come from?" I asked. "And where does it go?"

"Explaining magic is like explaining lightning or

rainbows a thousand years ago, inexplicable and wonderful but seemingly impossible. Today they are little more than equations in a science textbook. Magic is the fifth fundamental force and is even more mysterious than gravity, which is *really* saying something. Magic is a power lurking in all of us, an emotional energy that can be used to move objects and manipulate matter. But it doesn't follow any physical laws that we can, as yet, understand; it exists only in our hearts and minds."

"And the Dragonlands? What do they have to do with it?"

"I wish we knew. But one thing is crucial. With the way the power of magic has been deteriorating over the past fifty years, this happening — whatever it is — might be the last chance to regather the power before it goes completely."

"What are the chances it will happen?"

"A renewal is a risky undertaking. Chances are twenty percent at best." And on that note, Moobin returned to his tidying.

I looked at Mr. Stamford, who fired from his fingertip a shimmering globe that buzzed around the room before vanishing. He held up a hand-held shandarmeter, and I looked over his shoulder as the small needle bobbed against the scale.

"The background wizidrical radiation has risen almost tenfold since yesterday," he mused. "I've never seen anything quite like it. It's like we're . . . I don't know . . . moths to a light."

I wandered up to my room soon after, deep in thought. From my west-facing window, I watched the deep orange sun sink slowly behind the marzipan refinery at Sugwas, the heat from the refinery's gas flares wobbling the air and distorting the image. I sat down on the bed.

"Do you want some pizza, Tiger?"

"Yes, please," came a small voice from inside the wardrobe. It seemed Tiger still wasn't comfortable sleeping on his own. "Hey," he added, "is this a Matt Grifflon poster you've hidden in here?"

"I'm looking after it for a friend," I said hurriedly.

"Right."

NINETEEN

His Majesty King Snodd IV

I left Zambini Towers as soon as it was dark enough to move around without being spotted and spent the night at the Dragonstation. The crowds of press hadn't gone by the morning, and pretty soon I had to leave the phone off the hook. Two radio stations, the lifestyles section of the *Daily Mollusc,* the features editor of the *Clam,* and a representative from Fizzi-Pop all called me within the space of forty-seven seconds. All was not bad news, however. Gordon had outdone himself at breakfast, and I was soon tucking into a massive stack of pancakes. I was just reading in the paper about a border skirmish between the Kingdom of Hereford and the Duke of Brecon when there was a knock at the door.

"If it's that idiot from Yummy Flakes, tell him I'm dead," I said, not looking up from the newspaper. It wasn't the Yummy Flakes man. It wasn't even the theme park guy. It was a royal footman in full livery, who ignored Gordon and approached me at the breakfast table. He wore a pomaded wig, scarlet tunic, and breeches. His shirt had deep frilly cuffs, and his starched collar was so stiff he could barely move his head.

"Miss Strange?" he asked in a thin voice.

"Yes?"

"Dragonslayer?"

"Yes, yes?"

"I am commanded by His Majesty King Snodd to convey you to the castle."

"The castle? Me? You're joking!"

The footman looked at me coldly. "The king doesn't make jokes, Miss Strange. On the rare occasion that he does, he circulates a memo beforehand to avoid any misunderstandings. He has sent his own car."

The footman and chauffeur looked at me dubiously as the Quarkbeast joined me on the buzonji-hide-upholstered rear seat of the king's Hispano-Suiza K6 limousine, but they didn't say a word. We drove out of Hereford toward Snodd Hill, traditionally the place of residence for the monarch of Hereford since the Dragonpact, as it nestled comfortably—and strategically—against the eastern edge of the Dragonlands and was thus protected from attack in at least one direction. The high ramparts and curtain walls grew larger as we rattled over drawbridges on our way to the inner bailey.

I didn't have time to ponder much as the car pulled up outside the keep; the door was opened by another footman in impeccable dress. He beckoned me to follow, and I almost had to run to keep up as we negotiated the winding stairs of the old castle. After a brief sprint, he stopped outside two large wooden doors, knocked, and then flung them open with a flourish.

The doors led into a large medieval hall. The high ceilings were decorated with heraldic shields, and from the massive oak beams hung tapestries depicting the kingdom's dubiously won military triumphs over the centuries. At the far end of the room was a large fireplace, in front of which were two sofas that seated six men. They were all watching a young man outlining something on a blackboard. None of them seemed to take the least notice of me, so I walked closer, listening intently.

" . . . The trouble is," said the young man at the blackboard, who I recognized as His Gracious Majesty King Snodd IV, "that I have no idea what that rascal Brecon is up to. My sources tell me . . ."

His voice trailed off as he noticed me. I suddenly felt very small and naked as all the high lords of the kingdom swiveled their heads to stare at me. I knew most of them by sight, of course — they quite liked to get on TV. One in particular was on our screens more than the rest — Sir Matt Grifflon, recording artist and Hereford's most eligible bachelor, who was about as handsome as any man could be. He smiled at me, and I felt my heart flutter. Despite this, there was an uneasy silence. The men on the sofa were all clearly military men, although the only one I could recognize for sure was the Earl of Shobdon; Kazam had once charmed all the moles off his estate.

"Who are you?" demanded the king.

"Your servant, my lord," I stammered, curtsying clumsily. "My name is Jennifer Strange; I am the Dragonslayer."

"The Dragonslayer?" echoed the king. "The Dragonslayer is a *girl?*" I watched silently as he chortled with small grunty coughs. I had taken a dislike to my king already. As the others started to laugh, too, I felt a hot flush of anger rising under my skin. The king lifted a hand, and the laughter stopped. But before he could continue, his eyes opened wide, and he yelled out in alarm, "What in Snodd's name is *that?*"

It was the Quarkbeast. Bored with hiding behind a pillar, he had trotted out to sniff at the bronze leg of a table. The king quickly recovered and clapped his hands in delight.

"My goodness! A real live Quarkbeast!" He snapped

his fingers, and a footman appeared. "Some meat for the Quarkbeast. A *most* unusual pet, Miss Strange. Where did you find him?"

"Well, it was more of a case of him — "

"How *fascinating!*" replied the king. "You are loyal to the crown?"

"Yes, my lord."

"That's a relief. Tell me, Miss Dragonslayer, do you have an apprentice yet?"

"Yes, my lord, I do." The king walked closer, and I found myself backing away. I had to stop when I backed against a column, and he regarded me minutely through a monocle that he had screwed into his eye.

"Hmm," he said at last. "You will fire your apprentice and hire the man I send to you. That is all. You are dismissed."

I started to leave but then realized that my sixty-second accelerated Dragonslayer course had furnished me with one or two snippets about despots and how to deal with them. Instead of hurrying off, tail between legs and heartily intimidated, I stood my ground.

"You are dismissed!" the king repeated. "Are you deaf, girl? Away with you! Shoo!"

"My lord," said I, my voice cracking as I stared into the beetroot-red face of the monarch, "I wish only to serve my king and will do anything that he reasonably expects of me. But I must point out that by the Mighty Shandar's decree and ancient law, the concerns of the Dragonslayer are of no consequence to my noble king."

There was a deathly hush. One of the men started to giggle but wisely changed it into a cough. The king's monocle dropped from his face. He turned to his advisors and asked in an exasperated tone, "Was that a refusal?"

His aides muttered to one another, nodded, and generally made noises of assent. The king turned back to me and wagged a slender index finger in my face.

"You dare to speak of a higher authority than I? Where, might I ask, is this so-called Mighty Shandar? He has not been seen for four hundred years, yet you tell me that he has the last word on dragons? You are in big trouble, young lady."

"No, my lord, I think she does you greater honor by her refusal." The voice was raw and gravelly and spoke like the janitor from the convent. One of the king's advisors rose from the sofa, transplanting one of a pair of greyhounds that had been asleep at his feet, and approached us both.

"What is the meaning of this, Lord Chief Advisor?" the king demanded.

The lord chief advisor was a tall man of advancing years. His hair and beard were snow white, and he walked with a limp. He smiled at me, and I breathed a sigh of relief. It stood to reason that a king had others to advise him who were, well, *smarter*.

"I remember the last Dragonslayer, my lord. Perhaps you do not."

"*Previous* Dragonslayer," I said, interrupting without thinking.

"What?" said the king.

"Previous Dragonslayer. *I'm* the Last Dragonslayer, so if you mean Mr. Spalding, you should say previous Dragonslayer."

The king and lord chief advisor stared at me in disbelief. I don't think anyone had ever spoken out of turn in the king's presence. Or at least, not until now.

"We could have said *last* Last Dragonslayer," said the king.

"But it doesn't quite *sound* right, does it?"

The king stared at me for a long time, as likely as not contemplating execution. "Perhaps," he said at last, "but what is beyond doubt is that you, like the previous Dragonslayer, are grossly impertinent."

"There is a reason for that," intervened the lord chief advisor in his most diplomatic voice. "A Dragonslayer has a position quite unique. They are answerable not to one leader but to all of them. The independence of the Dragonslayer should not be compromised and never coerced."

"Speak English, damn you! Besides, who's coercing?" asked the king in a shocked tone. "I am ordering her to employ an apprentice of my choosing. It is *quite* a different matter. Guards, lock this Dragonslayer up in the most frightful room of the highest tower and feed her on powdered mouse until she agrees."

"You cannot, my lord."

"Cannot?" asked the king, his face again growing red with anger. "*Cannot?* I am the king. I WILL BE OBEYED!"

"As powerful as my lord is, not even your finest squadron of superdreadnought landships can come close to the power of magic."

"Magic? Pah!" scoffed the king. "This is the twenty-first century, Lord Chief Advisor. I think you give too much credence to antiquated notions."

But the lord chief advisor was not going to be defeated. "Your father never dismissed magic so readily, and neither should you."

The young king bit his lip and looked at me. The lord chief advisor continued, "I do not advise you to hold a Dragonslayer against her will, sire. I also think you should apologize to Miss Strange and welcome her to the court."

"What?!" said the king, his monocle popping out of his eye again. "Outrageous!"

At that moment the footman arrived with a small plate of meat for the Quarkbeast.

"What's that for?" asked the king, who had forgotten all about it.

"Quark," said the Quarkbeast, who hadn't. The footman placed the plate on the floor next to the Quarkbeast, who looked at me obediently. I nodded, and he demolished the food, then chewed the pewter plate before spitting it out in such a mangled and ugly state that one of the knights fainted and had to be carried out.

"Goodness," said the king, who had apparently never seen a Quarkbeast eat before. The greyhounds had seen, too, and wisely scurried away to hide.

The lord chief advisor took advantage of the distraction and leaned forward, whispering something in the king's ear for about thirty seconds. The king's face gradually broke into a smile.

"Oh, I see. Of course. Will do." The king turned to me again, and his manner had abruptly changed.

"I am so sorry, my dear. Please accept my apologies for my brusque behavior. No doubt you will have heard about the border skirmishes with the Duke of Brecon early this morning. Intelligence sources tell me that since your surprise appointment yesterday and the realization that this dragon chappie will soon be dead, Lord Brecon is considering moving his troops forward to capture as much of the Dragonlands as he can. I fully appreciate your position in all this, and I hope I can trust in your loyalty to Hereford?"

I was suspicious about his rapid about-face but decided not to show it. "You can, my lord."

"Perhaps you would consider a small request that I have in mind, then?"

"And that is — ?"

He shook his head sadly. "No, no, no. I am the king. You say yes, *then* ask me what I require. Your upbringing is not good, girl."

"Very well," I returned. "I will consider very carefully any request my king might make of me."

"A *bit* better," conceded the king doubtfully. "You realize that only you can get into the Dragonlands?"

I nodded.

"Good. I should like you to stake the claim of this crown all over the Dragonlands. So when the good dragon dies, your monarch and state will be in a more powerful position to better serve its citizens. In return for this, I offer you one hundred acres of the Dragonlands and the title Lady Jennifer, First Marchioness of Craswall. Am I not the most generous king ever?"

"I will consider what you have said most carefully, my lord."

"That's all agreed, then. Lord Chief Advisor, would you show this good lady to my car?"

The royal advisor took me by the arm, and we backed away together for a respectable distance before turning our backs on the king and leaving the room.

"I am Lord Tenbury, Miss Strange," announced the advisor in a kindly tone. "You may call me Tenbury. I was an advisor to the king's father. You will forgive King Snodd's quick temper." We continued to walk along the corridor, the Quarkbeast at our heels.

"You have trouble with the Duke of Brecon?" I asked him.

"As usual," he sighed. "Brecon would dearly love to expand into the Dragonlands as soon as Maltcassion dies, and I'm afraid we can't allow that to happen. You and your apprentice have the only access to the Dragonlands, and that is very useful to us. I beg you to consider the king's request most carefully." He stopped and looked earnestly into my eyes. "Remember that you are a subject of King Snodd, Jennifer, and that your duty as a Dragonslayer is second only to your duty as a loyal defender of this crown."

"All I want is what's best for the dragon, Tenbury."

The advisor smiled. "Things are never as simple as they appear, Miss Strange. By taking on the mantle of Dragonslayer, you have inherited a political position every bit as delicate as a skilled court advisor. I hope in all this you will make the right decisions." We had reached the front door, where the mute driver with the Hispano-Suiza awaited me.

"There is one other thing I would ask of you," said Tenbury, looking around nervously and moving closer.

"I respect your candor, sir," I replied. "What do you wish?"

"That you think very carefully about merchandising."

"What?"

"Merchandising. Dragonslayer toys, games, and so forth. It's big business these days; King Snodd's Useless Brother and I are regional representatives of Consolidated Useful Stuff and have been authorized to offer you twenty percent of everything sold. We think that plastic swords are probably worth a half million in sales alone." He smiled and gave me his card. "Promise me you'll think about it?"

"I will promise you that."

Up until that point, I had almost liked him. I sighed deeply. King Snodd's rapid about-face meant only one thing: I hadn't heard the last from him.

Yogi Baird

W hat did the king have to say?" asked Gordon van Gordon, who was doing the dishes in a flowery apron. He had taken off his suit jacket and rolled up his sleeves but was still wearing his brown derby hat.

"My elevation yesterday to Dragonslayer has removed any doubt that Maltcassion isn't long for this world. Brecon is looking to increase his lands, and the king is unwilling to let him do so. They want us to lay out the crown's claims on the Dragonlands before he dies, thus allowing the land to move painlessly into Snodd's hands."

"I see," said Gordon, "and what are your opinions on these matters?"

"I'm a Dragonslayer," I replied, "not a real estate agent. It won't make me very popular with the king, though."

"I agree with that. But you must do what you feel is right. Want a cup of tea?"

I nodded gratefully and followed him through to the kitchen.

"We had another call from Fizzi-Pop," he told me.

"Oh, yes?"

"They upped their offer to fifty thousand for your endorsement."

"What about Yummy Flakes?"

"They only went as far as forty. ConStuff wants to talk some more about merchandising rights, Cheap & Cheerful wants to launch a line of Jennifer Strange sport clothes, and ToyStuff wants a license to release a model of the Slayermobile. The bookies won't take any bets for you to win, but they are offering the dragon three hundred to one, and a tie at five hundred to one."

"Is that all?"

Gordon smiled, finished filling the kettle, and plugged it in. "No. MolluscTV wants to do a documentary about you, and the UKBC's wildlife department is interested in your taking a camera into the Dragonlands. I've had three producers wanting to buy the exclusive rights to your story, and one even said that Sandy O'Cute was very big on the idea of playing you in the movie."

"I bet she was."

"Out of your mail, ninety-seven percent want you to kill the dragon and three percent want you to leave it alone. Fifty-eight people have written in with offers of marriage, and two have claimed they are the real Dragonslayer. One little old lady in Chepstow wants you to use your sword to dispose of a particularly invasive thorn tree, and another in Cirencester wants you to appear at a fundraiser for the Troll War Orphans Appeal. And finally the Wessex Rolls-Royce club wants you to bring the Slayermobile to a car show next month."

"And this is just the beginning," I murmured.

Gordon poured the boiling water into the teapot. "It'll calm down, as soon as there's no more news."

"I hope. Milk, please, and half a sugar. Mind you, I'm not averse to appearing for the Troll War Orphans Appeal."

The doorbell rang. Gordon looked at his watch and pulled off his apron. "That'll be *The Yogi Baird Daytime TV Show.* Mother Zenobia arranged for you to talk to them."

"She did, didn't she?"

Gordon opened the door, and Yogi Baird strode in, shook my hand, and grinned wildly, saying how *wonderful* it was to meet me and how he simply *knew* it would be a great show. As he was telling me this, he was being dabbed at by a makeup woman. They were joined by a cameraman, an engineer, two electricians, a producer, two PAs, and someone in black whose function was to requisition our telephone and then make lots of calls about nothing in particular. Within a short time, they had the camera set up and a live uplink to a local transmitter. The same makeup person fussed over me as they set up two chairs in front of the spiky Rolls-Royce and a sound engineer fixed me up with a microphone.

While this all was going on, I had quietly placed a paper bag over the head of the Quarkbeast, with a single hole for him to see out. It wouldn't do to frighten the crew, and if the Quarkbeast went on live TV, he might cause a panic and small children would start crying, something neither of us wanted.

The floor manager counted Mr. Baird in with his fingers and pointed at him as the red "live" light mounted on top of the camera flicked on. The TV host grinned broadly.

"Good afternoon. This is Yogi Baird, speaking to you live from the Dragonstation in Hereford, capital city of the kingdom by the same name. In just a minute, we'll be talking to our very special guest, Dragonslayer Jennifer Strange. But before all that, a word from our sponsors. Has your get-up-and-go got up and went? Need a pick-me-up for a hard morning's work?" He produced a packet of breakfast cereal. "Then you need to try Yummy Flakes for that extra *vavoom!*"

He put down the packet as the jingle played briefly, then smiled into the camera and continued. "Listen, everyone's talking about dragons these last few days. Dragon this, dragon that, seems like a bit of a *drag* to me. That joke will *slay* me, but listen, folks . . ."

He didn't seem so funny live. The audience back at the studio were probably holding their sides, but I was uncomfortable. Like almost everyone in the kingdoms, I had watched the Yogi Baird show all my life, but was beginning to feel as though Dragonslayers should show more dignity. I stayed for Mother Zenobia's sake. I knew she would be watching—or listening, anyway.

" . . . Have you noticed just how many people have converged on the Dragonlands? Biggest show in town. Maltcassion will soon have his own TV station." The cameraman zoomed out to include me in the shot as the floor manager waved frantically at me to be ready.

" . . . But all kidding aside, for the past few days the small kingdom of Hereford has been alive with speculation over the death of the world's last dragon. With rumors of his demise imminent, this four-hundred-year-old Dragonland may soon be passed to any number of lucky claimants. I have with me the one person who could be battling the dragon sometime in the next week. Ladies and gentlemen, Jennifer Strange."

It was my first proper interview. I looked across at Gordon, who gave me a thumbs-up through the glare of the lights. I was being beamed live into more than thirty million homes. Two days ago no one had heard of me, yet today you would be hard pressed to find someone who hadn't. The power of the media.

"Welcome to the show, Jennifer."

"Thank you."

"Miss Strange, have you met with Maltcassion today?"

"Yesterday," I replied.

"And was he as horribly grotesque as you had thought?"

"No, on the contrary, I found him a highly intelligent creature."

"But ugly, of course? And potentially a man eater, with nothing on his mind but death and destruction?"

"Not in the least."

Yogi Baird abandoned that line of questioning. "Oh . . . kay. Even pre-cogs as low as B-3 are receiving visions that he is shortly to be killed at your hands. What's your reaction to that?"

"I can't say. Maltcassion has not transgressed the Dragonpact, and so long as he doesn't, I am not required or empowered to do anything at all. In fact," I added, "I think the name Dragonslayer is a misnomer. I see myself more as a keeper, who has to weigh the interests of the dragon against dangerous outside influences. Besides, we know very little about these noble creatures. I am in a good position to change all that. I aim to study Maltcassion."

"Ah, yes. Some newspapers have criticized you for your pro-dragon stance. Our researchers have uncovered the truth about dragons and they are, I quote: 'Dangerous fire-breathing and evil-smelling loathsome vermin who would think nothing of torching an entire village and eating all the babies were it not for the magic of the Dragonpact.'"

"Where did you read *that?*"

"My researchers have sources."

"Well," I conceded, "it *is* the populist view, although after my short meeting with Maltcassion, I was more inclined to think him a gentleman of considerable learning."

"So, loathsome worm or learned gentlemen? Let's see what the callers have to say. I have Millie Barnes on line one. Hello, Millie, what is your question, please?"

A little girl's voice came over the loudspeaker. She couldn't have been older than five.

"Hello, Jennifer. What's a dragon like?"

"He looks like a huge pile of stones, Millie. Rough and shapeless. You wouldn't know he was there unless he spoke. As for character, he is noble and fearless and has much that he could teach us —"

"Thank you for your question, Millie," said Mr.

Baird dismissively. "I have Colonel Baggsum-Gayme on three. Go ahead, Colonel."

"Jennifer, m'girl," said the colonel gruffly. "Best not to try and attack the blighter on your own, what with you being a girlie and all. Allow me to offer my services as the finest hunter of big game, advice absolutely free as long as I can stuff the ruffian and put him in the trophy room. I'll even have one of his legs made into an umbrella stand for you. Deal?"

"Next caller?" I asked.

"Hello, yes, I think what you're doing is absolutely right, and you should follow your own obviously high moral code in this most difficult of situations."

I liked this caller better. "Thank you, Mister—?"

"Strange. Or at least it will be. I think that I should adopt *your* name when we are married. Do you like Chinese food?"

Yogi Baird interrupted. "Thank you, caller. I have Mr. Savage from Worthing on line six. Hello, caller, go ahead."

"Hello, Miss Strange."

"Hello, Mr. Savage. What's your question?"

"You call yourself a Dragonslayer, Miss Strange, but I have irrefutable evidence, shown to me by a man in the pub, that it is I who am the true Dragonslayer. I see you as a usurper, keeping me from my true calling."

"Well, Mr. Savage," I began, thinking how wrong I had been to think that I would get only one nut case during the call-in, "perhaps you and I should discuss this *inside* the Dragonlands. As you know, only a true — " But the line had gone dead.

"Our next caller is Miss Shue from the Corporate Kingdom of Financia. Hello, caller, go ahead."

"Hello, yes. My husband is up at the Dragonlands, waiting for this creature to die, and we want to claim a small hill overlooking a stream. I wonder if you can tell us the best place to go once the force field is down?"

"My advice to you," I began slowly, "is the same for every person who might be waiting up at the Dragonlands."

"Yes?" said Yogi Baird expectantly.

"Go home. No matter what prophecy you've heard, the dragon has done nothing wrong. He is fit and well and will doubtless last for years." I suddenly felt very angry. "What is the matter with you people? A noble beast may die, and all you are thinking about is lining your own pockets! You're like a bunch of vultures hopping around a wounded zebra, waiting to poke your head into the rib cage and greedily pluck out a piece of — " I was almost shouting by now but stopped when one of the TV lights popped.

"That's it!" said the engineer, looking up from his mixing panel. "They've pulled the plug. We're off-air."

Yogi pulled his earpiece out and glared at me. "I have *never* been pulled on a live program before, Miss Strange! Who do you think you're talking to? This is *my* show and I like to keep it light. You want to get on a soapbox? Go on *Tonight with Clifford Serious*."

"But —"

He hadn't finished. "I've been on TV for twenty years, so I think my opinions count for something! Let me give you some advice: Act a bit more responsible in front of thirty million people. The bosses at Yummy Flakes are not going to be pleased. If I knew you were a troublemaker, I would have interviewed Sir Matt Grifflon instead. At least he has a song he's promoting!"

"Yogi darling!" yelled his producer, holding the telephone, "I've got the Zebra Society on the phone. They think we're negatively portraying zebras as passive victims. Will you have a word? They're a bit upset."

Baird glared at me.

"And I've got the Vulture Foundation on line two. They think your program is spreading unfair stereotypes about a noble bird."

"See what you've done? A few badly placed words in this business, and it's curtains. Ratings are everything — how could you be so selfish?" Yogi Baird turned and took the phone from his producer.

"No, sir," I heard him say. "I simply *adore* zebras . . ."

TWENTY-ONE

Foundling Trouble

I walked back to Zambini Towers, the Quarkbeast ensuring easy passage. There seemed to be a buzz in the city. The influx of people eager to stake a claim had been huge, and all the storekeepers were doing a roaring trade, keeping those in constant vigil up by the Dragonlands well stocked with food, bedding, and drink. String had long ago run out, and a consignment of ten thousand claim forms had been sold out in thirteen minutes.

Lady Mawgon was sitting in the lobby and looked as though she had been waiting to see me. "Miss Strange," she said, rising to meet me, "don't think that becoming a Dragonslayer has in any way altered the low opinion that

I hold of you and Master Prawns. Despite that frightful hag Zenobia refusing to supply us with any alternative foundlings, I have negotiated with the King of Pembroke to send us replacements. They arrive on Monday, so I will expect you to be packed and back at the Blessed Ladies of the Lobster by Monday lunchtime." She glared at me with a triumphant grin.

"With the greatest of respect, my lady," I replied, "I believe only Mr. Zambini can sign our release papers."

"On the contrary," sneered Lady Mawgon, who had obviously been doing her homework, "the Minister for Foundling Affairs is King Snodd's Useless Brother, and he owes me a favor. He will oversign your papers." She smiled unpleasantly, but I wasn't out of ideas quite yet.

"I am acquainted with the king," I told her, "and he has charged me with an important task within the Dragonlands." This was true, of course. But I wasn't going to tell Lady Mawgon I'd refused the king's request to claim the Dragonlands in his name.

"Your influence ends at noon on Sunday," said Lady Mawgon, "the predicted time of the Dragondeath. After that, no one will much care what happens to you. The Useless Brother signs your return-to-orphanage papers on Sunday evening."

I stared at her hotly. There didn't seem to be much I could say.

"That wiped off your silly smirk, didn't it? And don't try to steal any silverware—I'll be searching you both as you leave."

"Miss Jennifer?" It was Tiger with a message.

"Yes?"

"There's been a news flash. The Duke of Brecon has raised an army to advance upon the Dragonlands as soon as the dragon is dead. They aim to claim most of the land for themselves. Every able-bodied man or woman in Brecon is to be mobilized."

A cold hand fell on my heart. I hadn't thought it would come to this so quickly. The Kingdom of Hereford and the Duchy of Brecon had been itching for a fight for years, and the size of their armies would make it potentially the biggest land battle fought in the kingdoms. Worse, I knew for a fact that King Snodd was dying to try out his superdreadnought landships, vast tracked vehicles of riveted steel seven stories high that crushed and destroyed all in their path.

"We haven't had a good war for years," said Lady Mawgon, "and never one on live TV. Colorful costumes, the clank of machinery, rousing songs. It will be most enjoyable."

"If your idea of enjoyment is watching people get killed in an unspeakably unpleasant way," replied Tiger sarcastically, "then I guess so."

"Your impertinence knows no bounds," remarked Lady Mawgon scornfully, "but since you will not be here for long, I shall ignore it. There won't be any death — it'll be a walkover. Brecon won't be able to muster more than five thousand troops. Hereford has a lot of seriously good military hardware and at least eighty thousand men — and that doesn't include the Berzerkers."

"King Snodd would use Berzerkers?" I asked.

"He would," replied Lady Mawgon. "Nothing like the sight of a Berzerker in a crazed frenzy to get the enemy to beg for peace."

I was shocked. Berzerkers were highly unstable individuals possessed of such grossly volatile temperaments that they fought with extraordinary powers. In every civilized nation they were defined within the Geneva Convention as "illegal weapons of war that could cause unnecessary suffering and injury."

"Would you excuse me, Lady Mawgon? I have to make a telephone call."

She inclined her head to dismiss us, and we hurried off toward the offices.

"Here." I handed Tiger a signed photo of Yogi Baird. "I was going to tear this up into small pieces but thought you might like to instead."

"That's very thoughtful of you," said Tiger. "Did Lady Mawgon tell you about us being replaced?"

"That's not until Monday," I said. "Lots can happen."

"I don't want to go back to the Sisterhood."

"It won't come to that, I promise."

I wished I could believe it. The rights that foundlings possessed could be written on an ant in quite large letters. I was in no doubt that Mawgon could do precisely as she said, and there was nothing we could do to stop her.

"Think that's small enough?" asked Tiger, showing me the torn-up picture of Yogi Baird.

"That part there," I said, pointing out a piece that could be smaller still. I dialed the number Lord Tenbury had given me and was soon through to the switchboard at Snodd Hill castle.

"I'd like to speak to the king, please."

"I'm sorry," said a snotty receptionist with a plummy voice, "the king doesn't take person-to-person calls."

"Tell him it's Jennifer Strange."

A few minutes later the king came on the line. "I don't make a habit of using the phone, Miss Strange," he announced loftily, "but since it is you, I will be willing to make an exception. You wish to tell me you will lay claim to the lands for me?"

"You cannot go to war over the Dragonlands," I said, all royal protocol now vanished. There was silence for a few moments.

"Cannot?" questioned the king. "Cannot? It is *your* fault that tempers me to this extremity, my dear. If you had made claim to the lands as we requested, then none of this would be necessary. Brecon amasses his troops at the border, so we must meet force with force."

"But the dragon is not going to die. He has done nothing wrong!"

"The court soothsayer Sage O'Neons is rarely mistaken, my dear. Are you willing to lay claim to the Dragonlands for the crown?"

"Will it stop the battle?"

"Sadly, no. It will merely give us the benefit of international law being on our side."

"Then I gain nothing. I refuse." Royal politics was not something I was good at.

But the king had other ideas. "There is something you *can* do to avert serious loss of life even now."

"What?"

"You can kill the dragon earlier than expected. Our spies tell us Brecon is unprepared; we can sweep across the lands before he even realizes it. Dead dragon now, dead dragon later, what's the difference? How about Saturday at teatime? Do we have a deal?"

"No."

"I will make you a rich girl, Miss Strange. Richer than you can imagine. I will raise your title to Baroness

Strange of Hay and make you junior minister for traffic. I will pledge fifty thousand moolah to the Troll War Widows Fund. What do you say?"

"My answer is the same."

"Very well. I was talking just recently to my Useless Brother. He tells me that you have . . . political problems over at Kazam. Do what I ask, and I shall release you and your assistant from your indentured servitude. You will both be citizens, my dear."

I went silent. I had only two years to go, but Tiger had six. I looked across at him, but he was busy doing the filing.

"I'm waiting for your answer, Miss Strange," said the king. "I am a generous man, but also an impatient one. Cash, freedom, and a title. What will it be?"

"No," I said at last.

"*What?*"

"The life of a dragon is not for sale at any price — not even for freedom. It is due to *your* intransigence that Troll War widows are reduced to begging at all. I reject your offer and will never compromise my position as Last Dragonslayer to assist your military conquests. Not now, not ever."

There was silence for a moment. "You disappoint me, my dear. I hope you will not regret your decision."

The line went dead. I looked up to find Tiger staring at me. "Did you just turn down an offer of him lifting your servitude?"

"No," I said, feeling a bit stupid. "I turned it down for both of us."

"Hmm," he said after a moment's thought. "I hope this dragon friend of yours is worth it."

"I don't know," I said. "The Mighty Shandar's recorded message told me not to trust men *or* dragons. I know I can't trust Snodd and the Earl of Tenbury. Brian Spalding is dead and Mr. Zambini indisposed. The only thing to trust is my own gut feeling, and that tells me Maltcassion is the one to follow. If I'm wrong, I apologize now."

"No apology necessary," replied Tiger cheerfully. "Sister Assumpta bet me a moolah I wouldn't last a week at Kazam, but aside from that, I would only be back where I started." He was taking it quite well, all things considered.

"I need to somehow level the playing field," I said, mostly to myself. "War can always be averted — you just have to find out how."

"You know what you should do?"

"Strike Lady Mawgon on the back of the head with a cabbage?"

"A fine idea — but I was thinking you should speak

to the Duke of Brecon and tell him his army is seriously outnumbered and outgunned."

"Tricky," I said, "not to mention treasonous. I preferred the cabbage idea. But you're right. The problem is, how? All the phone lines between the two states were cut years ago, and the border is closed."

"Jenny," said Tiger, "what does a Dragonslayer care about borders?"

TWENTY-TWO

Conversation with Moobin

To maintain a low profile, I waited until evening and then drove up to the Dragonlands in my Volkswagen. Wizard Moobin and Mr. Stamford were with me, eager to see for themselves the spectacle of almost a million people waiting for Maltcassion to die.

"Any developments?" I asked as we drove across the River Wye.

Moobin showed me the shandarmeter. The needle was almost off the scale.

"More magic?"

"And how. Every hour that passes, the meter jumps another five hundred shandars."

"Where is it coming from?"

"It seems," said the wizard, "to be centered on the Dragonlands."

I had a thought. "How much power do you need to start Big Magic?"

"I don't know."

"Make a guess."

"At *least* ten gigashandars."

"And at this rate, when would you expect the combined wizidrical energy to exceed that?"

"Yes," he said, getting my drift, "Sunday around noon."

"The time of the predicted Dragondeath. Don't tell me it's all a coincidence."

"I think not," replied Moobin. "But all that energy has to come from *somewhere*. There aren't ten gigashandars of power on the planet. The most generous estimate of the world's power is barely five, and that includes the power locked up in those marker stones. Even with every magician on the planet, we'd still be at least three gigashandars short. I think the rate of increase will level out and leave us short by a long way. And even if we do get ten gigs of power around the Dragonlands, no one's sure how we might be able to channel it."

"We've still got a couple of days."

"Would you look at that . . ." murmured Mr. Stamford, staring out the window. We followed his gaze to where rows of colossal tracked machines of riveted iron and steel stood silent against the night sky, their substantial bulk brought into sharp relief by the large floodlights that illuminated the edge of the Dragonlands.

"Landships," said Moobin in a quiet voice.

King Snodd meant business. Each landship was capable of carrying two hundred soldiers and enough firepower to attack even the most robust defenses. But despite appearances, they weren't invincible. Many lives had been lost in those towers of iron during the disastrous campaign that became known as the Fourth Troll War.

We said nothing more as we approached the Dragonlands, and I threaded the car between parking lots, military outposts, hamburger trucks, and television vans. Most of all, we noticed the people—more people than I had ever seen in one place before, nor ever would again. They were all ready and waiting, holding stakes, mallets, and lengths of string, in case the dragon died early and the force field fell. All that was required to claim land was to enclose a section and peg a claim form to the grass with your name and signature. It was part of the Dragonpact.

I drove as close as I dared, not wanting to attract attention. The area was being patrolled by members of the elite Imperial Guard. I turned to Moobin and Mr. Stamford.

"You both better get out. I'm going into the Dragonlands."

They needed no further bidding and clambered out, wishing me good luck in whatever I was about to do. I thanked them and accelerated toward an unguarded piece of land between the marker stones. Suicide by force field was not uncommon, and I suppose this was what most people thought I was up to as I passed, amid frenzied shouts, between the marker stones and into the Dragonlands. They would have realized who I was as I drove on, but I was soon lost to view, bumping across the turf in the darkness. I drove over a rise and was soon within the relative quiet of the Dragonlands.

A full moon had risen. I didn't think I would have much trouble finding my way to where the land bordered the sworn enemy of the King of Hereford: the Duke of Brecon.

TWENTY-THREE

The Duke of Brecon

The Duchy of Brecon was a place I had never visited. Stories of the iniquity of the Duke of Brecon were common in the kingdom, and I was taking no chances against the duke's possible treachery. As soon as I thought I had driven far enough, I descended the hill and came within sight of more floodlights, crowds, and military. These were Brecon's troops, who were very surprised to see me but soon guessed who I was. Most people watched the same news channels, and *The Yogi Baird Daytime TV Show* was syndicated everywhere.

"I wish to meet with the Duke of Brecon," I said to an officer who came running up once I had parked my Volkswagen.

"I shall take you to him, gracious Dragonslayer," said the officer, bowing low.

"No," I replied, staying safely behind the buzzing marker stones, "I would be grateful if the duke would come to see me."

The officer told me that the duke didn't make house calls, but when he saw I was adamant, he ran off. I sat down on the grass and waited while the soldiers asked me what it was like to live in the Kingdom of Hereford, where they had heard the roads were paved with gold, cars were given away free with breakfast cereals, and a man could make a million moolah in a year selling string. I tried to put them right.

It wasn't long before they all drew apart as a tall man dressed in a heavy greatcoat walked up the hill toward us. He had with him three aides-de-camp, all dressed in the costume of the Breconian Royal Guard. The foot soldiers were cleared back so we could talk in private, and for a moment the duke and I stood there, facing each other across the humming boundary. One of the aides-de-camp took it upon himself to make a formal announcement.

"May I present his worshipfulness, his worthiness, his beauteous — "

"That's enough!" The Duke of Brecon smiled in a kindly fashion. "Miss Strange, I am at your service. Please join me." He clicked his fingers, and two chairs and a table were carried up and placed upon the grass. The table was set with a candelabrum and a bowl of fruit.

"Please!" he said, indicating a chair.

Suspicious, I stayed behind the boundary marker where he could not reach me. He nodded and strode over to where I was standing, tossed some dust into the barrier to see where it was, and held out his hand just inches from the force field.

"Then allow me to shake the hand of the Last Dragonslayer?"

Almost instinctively, I put my hand through the force field and grasped his. It was a mistake. He pulled me through to his side of the boundary, and I cursed myself for falling for such a stupid trick. I expected to be captured, but instead the duke released me.

"You are free to return, Miss Strange. I only did that to show that you could trust me." Not one of his people moved as Brecon sat at the table. "Come," he said. "Sit with me, and we will talk like civilized human beings."

From television reports and the papers, I had always supposed him to be an ogre of a man, but he seemed quite the opposite. Those news stations *were* Hereford- and state-controlled, so I reasoned there was a natural bias involved. I sat down.

"I take many risks in coming to see you, sire," I began. "I want to avoid war at all costs."

The duke tapped his fingers on the table. "Your king thinks poorly of me for wanting to expand my territory into the Dragonlands when Maltcassion passes on. He does not appreciate that my land is one-tenth the size of his and considerably poorer. But Snodd's designs are not wholly centered on the Dragonlands. He has been looking for a good reason to invade my country for years. If a battle starts on the Dragonlands, it will only end one way for me: the invasion of our territory and an end to the Duchy of Brecon. Wales is suffering disunity at present and would be a walkover for King Snodd. I would expect this to be the first step in an invasion of the entire nation. Snowdonia might put up a fight, but Hereford has many friends in the east who might willingly form an alliance. The tourism dollars of the mountainous nation alone are potentially worth billions."

"Invade Wales?" I repeated incredulously. I knew the king was warlike, but this seemed a little far, even for him. "He would never do that!"

"Alas, I think he might. You are too young to remember the previous king's annexation of the Monmouth Principality on the grounds of historical ownership, but I am not. Snodd is looking to increase and consolidate his lands, and I will not let him do it."

"I think you're wrong."

"He has thirty-two landships," remarked Brecon,

"when it would take only one to crush my small duchy. Think about it, Miss Strange."

Brecon's words had the ring of truth. It was thought that the King of Hereford simply liked having parades, but perhaps there was a more insidious reason for his love of military hardware.

"How will you react," I asked, "if the force field comes down?"

Brecon stared at me for a moment. "Come Maltcassion's demise, we do not aim to move into the Dragonlands at all."

"Then what are the soldiers for?"

"Defense," replied the duke, "pure and simple."

"Why are you telling me all this?" I couldn't understand why Brecon would give me delicate state secrets.

"I tell you because I know I can trust you. The Dragonslayer is a neutral party, belonging to no kingdom, making no decision for one dominion in favor of another. King Snodd appears a fool but is well advised—I suspect he has offered you inducements to help stake claims within the Dragonlands."

I thought of the promises that King Snodd had made me, the land and money and freedom and title in exchange for staking his claim. "So you will make me a better offer?" I asked, thinking naïvely that Snodd and Brecon were the same fleas on a different Quarkbeast.

"No," asserted the duke. "I offer you nothing and will pay you nothing. Not one Breconian groat. I simply ask you to abide by the rules of your calling."

We shook hands on it. I liked Brecon a great deal. As I turned to walk back into the Dragonlands, I noticed that several excavators were starting to build large ditches to defend against the expected invasion on Sunday afternoon. It would be a waste of time. Landships would pass over them as if they were not there. Brecon had nothing compared to the military might of King Snodd.

"It will be bows and arrows against the lightning," I told him.

"I know," replied Brecon sadly. "My artillery will barely dent the landships. But we will fight to maintain our freedom. I will be here, next to my men, defending my beloved country to the last shot in my revolver and the final breath in my body."

"I wish you luck, sire."

He thanked me but said nothing further. He had a lot of work to do.

I returned to the Dragonlands deep in thought. Right now I couldn't see anything but bad news in every direction. But then it struck me that everyone kept forgetting about Maltcassion himself, even though he was at the heart of everything. And the fact remained that the pre-cogs had spoken of a Dragondeath at the hand of a Dragonslayer. Destiny had me killing Maltcassion at noon on Sunday. But the fact of the matter was, if Maltcassion didn't transgress the Dragonpact, I didn't have to.

I slipped back to Zambini Towers to tell Tiger what had happened. More sorcerers and magicians had arrived, and a late-night party seemed to be going on. All the retired magicians of the land were making their way to the small kingdom, following an instinct to lend whatever power they had to the Big Magic.

TWENTY-FOUR

Dragonattack

I was awakened by Gordon van Gordon pulling on my sleeve and urging me to wakefulness. I had been dreaming of dragons again, but not all the dreams were good ones. Maltcassion had been looking at me with a grim expression, explaining what it meant to him to be a dragon, but I hadn't really been listening and missed something important, which annoyed me.

"What's that noise?" I asked.

"It's the red phone."

"I don't have a red phone. And what are you doing in Zambini Towers?"

"We're not at Zambini Towers." He was right. I was at the Dragonstation.

"Oh," I said, shaking the fog of sleep from my head and looking at the hotline phone that was ringing under its cake cover. "Don't worry, it'll probably be someone wanting a pizza. Benny's number is quite similar."

But it wasn't someone wanting a pizza. It was someone wanting a Dragonslayer.

Within ten minutes, the armored Rolls-Royce was heading south of the city. Gordon was driving because he needed more to do, I was fretting about what we would find, and the Quarkbeast was yawning and wondering why we were up so early.

The low sun was just spreading its rays across the land as we drove toward Longtown, a village right on the edge of the Dragonlands. POLICE LINE DO NOT CROSS tape was stretched across the road and Gordon parked the Rolls-Royce next to a large contingent of police cars. I introduced myself to a policewoman, who guided me among the many emergency personnel and news crews. The road underfoot was awash with water, and the number of fire appliances made me uneasy.

"We meet again, Miss Strange," said Detective Villiers, standing with Sergeant Norton. "I should arrest you right now for withholding evidence."

"I didn't know I was the Last Dragonslayer then."

"That's *your* story."

"Events have moved on," I told them. They looked me up and down.

"Kind of young for a Dragonslayer?" said Villiers finally.

I stared back at him. "Perhaps you tell me what's going on."

"We found the claw marks in the cab." He beckoned me to follow, and we walked toward a large ConStuff truck lying upended in a field. It had been completely gutted by fire, and the water used to extinguish the flames had run down the field and flooded the road with mud. Villiers pointed. On the bodywork, just below the roofline, were two large grooved holes, as though something very massive and very strong had simply squeezed the truck.

"Vandals?" I asked, somewhat dubiously.

Detective Villiers stared at me as though I were an imbecile. "Talons, Miss Strange, *talons*. This truck was taken from Gloucester last night and turned up here. When the firefighters arrived, they were positive there were no wheel tracks; if you look here"—he indicated an area of damage to the rear of the truck, which had been heavily caved in; the back axle had been almost torn off—"it looks as though the truck was dropped from a great height."

"So what are you saying?" I asked him.

"You tell me, Miss Dragonslayer. Looks to me as though Maltcassion picked up this vehicle and tried to fly with it back to the Dragonlands, but dropped it on the way. To try and disguise the crime, he torched it."

"A truck hardly counts as livestock, does it?"

"A technicality. The Dragonpact states damage of *property* as a punishable offense. I think what we got here is a rogue dragon."

"That's sort of far-fetched." I tried to play the incident down. It was a serious accusation. A rogue dragon was a dragon out of control, one that had transgressed the rules of the Dragonpact. Such a dragon could legally be destroyed. That's the trouble with premonitions; they have an annoying habit of coming true. "Did anyone see it?"

Villiers looked at his feet. "No."

"Anyone hear anything, see it being flown out here?"

"No."

"Then by the rules of the Dragonpact, I'm going to have to see at least two other uncorroborated incidents of Dragonattack before I can even consider this a rogue dragon."

Villiers turned on me angrily. "It's pretty clear-cut!"

"Then *you* punish him, Villiers," I returned. "I'm going to need to see better evidence than this."

I left Villiers and lifted the police tape and was instantly assailed by a wall of journalists.

"Was this an attack by a dragon?" asked a reporter from the *Daily Eyestrain.*

"Unlikely."

"How could you know it wasn't Maltcassion?"

"I didn't say it wasn't. I said it was *unlikely*."

"So you're confused?"

"No."

"Is it true," asked another pressman, "that you stated on the Yogi Baird show that you aim to study Maltcassion?"

"If I can."

"Then you have a vested interest in keeping the dragon alive?"

"What's this all about?"

"We're wondering whether you're qualified to make an objective decision on Dragondeath. Perhaps in light of your dubious conflict of interests, you had best leave Dragonslaying to someone else. We understand Sir Matt Grifflon has just held a press conference in which he stated his eagerness to assume your duties. Has he contacted you?"

I didn't answer. Another reporter took a turn as I walked in the direction of the Rolls-Royce.

"Sophie Trotter of the UKBC," announced the

reporter. "Miss Strange, does the prospect of having to carry out your duty fill you with trepidation?"

"It won't come to that."

"But if Maltcassion reneges on the Dragonpact, you will act to destroy him?"

"If he does, I will carry out my duty."

"Do you think King Snodd's declaration of no confidence in your abilities will make you reconsider your decision to resign?"

I stopped so fast, the pack of journalists nearly walked into the back of me. "King Snodd said that?"

"At Sir Matt Grifflon's press conference this morning. He called for your resignation and endorsed Sir Matt to take your place. Such an undertaking is allowed within the Dragonslayer's charter, we take it?"

"I can transfer my calling . . . but only to a *knight*," I murmured. I was being steadily outmaneuvered.

"So will you be resigning?"

"Listen," I replied somewhat testily, "I am the Last Dragonslayer. I will uphold the rule of law as laid down by the Dragonpact to the best of my abilities. I have no plans to do otherwise. Excuse me."

I climbed aboard the armored Rolls-Royce, and Gordon drove us away from the mob and headed back to town.

"Are you all right?" he asked.

"Sure. I was hoping to be able to study Maltcassion at my leisure; that hope is rapidly fading."

Gordon nodded in the direction of the truck. "What was all that about?"

"Villiers thinks it was a Dragonattack: talon marks on an eighteen-wheeler. Even if it was Maltcassion — which I doubt — it isn't enough to have him destroyed. If he does it several times, then I might have to do something. The good thing is that no one was killed. As long as no lives are lost, I can drag this beyond the prophecy deadline. Pre-cogs only see a version of the future. As soon as a deadline is missed, the prophecy becomes less and less likely."

"So who did this, if not Maltcassion?"

"Who knows? Both Hereford and Brecon have heavy-lift helicopters; either of them could have done it. The Dragonlands are of great strategic importance to them both. I've got no way of knowing who is telling the truth. Brecon says he doesn't want the land at all and is fearful of being invaded, whereas King Snodd is convinced that Brecon wants to take over the whole area. I don't know who to believe, so I've canceled them both out like opposite ends of an equation. I'll have to judge all this on merit as we go along."

I lapsed into silence as we drove back to the Dragonstation. There were a lot of reporters there, too, but I avoided them all as Gordon drove me straight inside. The news of my refusal to kill the dragon without corroboration spread quickly; I had to leave the phone off the hook after some unpleasant calls. A jeering mob started to yell outside the Dragonstation that I was a coward or something, which went on for an hour until some animal rights campaigners turned up on my behalf. There was a short battle, and the police waded in with water cannon and tear gas. I don't think anyone was hurt, but a brick came through the front window.

"Tea?" said Gordon with masterful good timing. "I've made a cake, too."

"Thank you."

TWENTY-FIVE

Mr. Hawker

I was reading *The Dragonslayer's Manual* over breakfast and had just come to the part about using a banana to sharpen Exhorbitus when there was a sharp rap at the door. I opened it to reveal a small man dressed in a worn suit. He was flanked by two huge police officers whose knuckles almost touched the ground.

"Yes?"

"Miss Strange, Dragonslayer?"

"Yes, yes?"

"My name is Mr. Hawker. I represent the Hawker and Sidderley Debt Collection Agency."

Hawker handed me a sheaf of papers, all headed with

the kingdom's judicial seal and looking terribly formal. I had no doubt that it was all official, very legal, and wholly dishonest.

"What does it mean?" I asked Hawker, who seemed to be enjoying himself.

"This property has been given rent free by the kingdom for almost four hundred years," he explained. "We have discovered that this was a clerical error."

"And you found out just this morning, I suppose?"

"Indeed. Back rent, back electrical bills, gas bills, rates, you name it. Four hundred years' worth."

"I've only been here two days."

Hawker — and the king's advisors, presumably — had already thought of that.

"As Dragonslayer, you are legally responsible for yourself and the previous members of your calling. The kingdom has been generous for many years but feels now that circumstances have changed." He looked at me with a smile. "You owe us 97,482 moolah and forty-three pence."

I had expected King Snodd to make life difficult, but not this way. I patted my pockets, drew out some change, and handed it to the debt collector, who wasn't laughing.

"Now how much do I owe you?"

"I think you fail to appreciate the seriousness of the

situation, Miss Strange. If you do not pay the monies owed, I have a warrant for your arrest. Failure to pay will result in being jailed for debt."

He obviously meant it. I could only assume that the king thought a brief stay in jail would make me more compliant. But I wasn't about to be arrested just like that. I asked Mr. Hawker to wait and called Gordon to fetch the accounts. Brian Spalding had said we had funds in the bank.

"How long do I have to pay?"

The debt collector smiled as one of the officers started cracking his knuckles.

"We're not totally devoid of a sense of fair play," replied Hawker with a gloat. "Ten minutes."

"Well?" I said to Gordon, who had returned with the bank statements.

"Not too good, ma'am," he said. "It seems we have a fraction under two hundred."

"Oh, dear," said Hawker. "Officers, arrest her." The policemen stepped forward, but I raised a hand.

"Wait!" They stopped. "I thought you said I had ten minutes?"

Hawker gave a rare smile and checked his watch. "Think you can raise a hundred thousand moolah in, let's see . . . eight minutes?"

"Well," I replied, "actually, I think I can."

TWENTY-SIX

Maltcassion Again

An hour later I was heading off to the Dragonlands again, the Rolls-Royce bedecked with Fizzi-Pop stickers. On the door was a big sign:

Dragonslayer
Officially sponsored by
Fizzi-Pop, Inc.
The Drink of Champions

Sometimes you have to do things you don't want to for the greater good. After Mr. Hawker's warning, I dashed out and collared the Fizzi-Pop representative, who had been camping outside the Dragonstation. He and his opposite at Yummy Flakes breakfast cereals had quickly called their bosses and bid over the phone for my endorsement of their product. Yummy Flakes had pulled out at M95,000, but Fizzi-Pop had gone all the way to my asking price of M100,000.

It was a simple deal: I was to wear their hat and jacket in public, and the Slayermobile had to be similarly adorned. I had to appear in five commercials and do nothing to impinge on the good name of the product. The alternative was debtor's prison, so I didn't have much choice. Hawker, as you might expect, was furious. He had called his lawyers and tried to find a way around the problem, but this was something they had not expected. It wasn't the end of it, I was sure, but at least it was the first round to me. And actually, I like Fizzi-Pop.

As I approached the Dragonlands I noted that even more people had gathered. Just behind the marker stones was now a five-hundred-yard-deep swath of tents, food trucks, toilets, marquees, first-aid stations, and parked cars. The word was spreading, and citizens were arriving from the farthest kingdoms of the land. It was rumored that claimants were arriving from the Continent and masquerading as citizens of the Ununited Kingdoms in order to stake a claim. A bus full of Danes had been detained in Oxford, a load of rollmop herrings having given them away.

As I drove along one of the access roads kept clear for deliveries of food and other essentials, ten thousand heads swiveled in my direction, and the buzz of conversation dropped to silence. The crowd parted to give me access to the marker stones, but this was probably less from respect than from the possibility of profit: I was key in the whole affair.

I bumped onto the Dragonlands and drove up the hill toward Maltcassion's lair. It was a beautiful day. Birds were busy building nests, and bees buzzed among the wildflowers, which grew in cheerful profusion on the unspoiled land. I found Maltcassion in the clearing that was his lair, the marker stone in the middle humming a bit louder than the last time. The old dragon was busy scratching his back against an old oak that bent and creaked under his weight.

"Hello, Miss Strange!" he said in a cheerful tone. "What brings you here?"

"To speak with you."

"Well, cheer up, old girl. Your face looks long enough to reach your feet!"

"You don't know what's going on out there!" I replied miserably, waving my hand in the direction of the outside world.

"Oh, but I do," replied Maltcassion. "You can see the visible spectrum of light, can't you? Violet to red, yes?"

I nodded and sat down on a stone.

"A pretty poor selection, I should think!" said the dragon, stopping his scratching, much to the relief of the oak tree. "I can see *much* further. At the slow end of the electromagnetic spectrum lie the languorous long radio waves that move like cold serpents. Next are the bright blasts of medium and short radio waves that occasionally burst from the sun. I can see the strange point sources of AM radio stations, like raindrops striking a pond. I can see the strange thermal images of low infrared, and beyond them the visible spectrum that we share; then we are off again, past blue and out beyond violet to ultraviolet. We go past google rays and manta rays and then to the curious world of the x-ray, where everything but the most dense materials are transparent. I can see all this, a beautiful and radiant world quite outside your understanding. But it's not all just for fun. You see this?"

He showed me one of his ears. It folded into a flap behind his eye and was of a delicate meshlike construction, like the ribs on a leaf. He unfurled it, rotated it, and then slotted it away again.

"A dragon's senses are far more keen than yours. I can see your television and radio signals. But more than that, I can *read* them. I can pick up sixty-seven TV channels and forty-seven radio stations. I thought you were great on *The Yogi Baird Daytime TV Show.*"

"How about cable?"

"Luckily, no."

"Then you heard about the incident this morning? The truck the police thought was you?"

"I heard something about that, yes. What I would be doing stealing eighteen-wheelers is anyone's guess; I don't even have a driver's license. Have you had lunch?"

"And you're not bothered?!" I jumped up, my voice rising. "There are crowds of people outside waiting for you to die so they can take over this haven! Doesn't that worry you?"

Maltcassion stared at me and blinked the lids above his jewellike eyes. "It bothered me once. I am old now and have been waiting for you for a number of years. But there is another place we can see. Not radio waves or gamma waves but another realm entirely—the cloudy subether of potential outcome."

"The future?"

"Ah, yes!" said Maltcassion, raising a claw in the air. "The future. The undiscovered country. We all journey there sooner or later. Don't let anyone tell you the future is already written. The best any prophet can do is give you the *most likely* version of future events. It is up to us to accept the future for what it is, or change it. It is easy to go with the flow; it takes a person of singular courage to go against it. It was long foreseen that the

Dragonslayer who oversaw the last of our kind would be a young woman of singular mind, remarkable talents, and generosity of spirit. She would set us free."

"Are you sure you've got the right Jennifer Strange?" I asked.

The dragon changed the subject abruptly. "There is more, but it's all so vague. I could remember it once, but there are so many thoughts in here that it's difficult to work out."

"You heard about King Snodd and the Duke of Brecon lining up for battle?"

"Yes. All is going to plan, Miss Strange."

"All to plan? This is your doing?"

"Not everything. You will have to trust me on this."

"But I don't understand."

"You will, little human, you will. Leave me. I shall see you Sunday morning — and don't forget your sword."

"I won't come!" I said as defiantly as you can in front of forty tons of dragon.

"Yes, you will," answered Maltcassion soothingly. "It is out of your hands as much as it is out of mine. Big Magic has been set in motion, and nothing will stop it."

"This is Big Magic? You, me, the Dragonlands?"

He shrugged in a very humanlike manner, which seemed vaguely comical.

"I know not. I cannot see beyond noon on Sunday;

there can be only one reason for that. Premonitions come true because people want them to. The observer will always change the outcome of an event; the millions of observers we have now will almost guarantee it. You and I are just small players in something bigger than either of us. Leave now. I will see you on Sunday."

Reluctantly, and with more questions than answers, I departed.

By the time I got back to Zambini Towers, there had already been fresh allegations about Maltcassion's supposed misdemeanors. I was called to the sites of both, one after the other. To avoid undue panic or being trailed around by the press, I took my car rather than the Slayermobile.

Detective Villiers was waiting for me on a side road near the village of Goodrich, where there were as many police cars and forensic teams as at the last supposed Dragonattack. This time, however, he was more confident: Villiers had what could only be described as a large smirk etched across his features.

"Try and tell me this wasn't a dragon!" he leered.

He led me past the police cordon and pointed at the ground. On the road was the sort of mark an overly hot iron might make on a shirt. The black scorch mark had left the clear imprint of a man in a spread-eagle pattern; I didn't like the look of it.

"Scorch mark, no body, classic sign of a dragon. *And*"—Villiers paused for dramatic effect—"I have a witness!" He introduced me to a wizened old man who smelled strongly of marzipan. He was eating the foul substance out of a paper bag and was unsteady in speech and limb.

"Tell the Dragonslayer what you saw, sir."

The old man's eyes flicked up to mine. He explained in a stammering voice about balls of fire and terrible noises in the night. He spoke of his friend being there one minute and gone the next. He showed me his scorched eyebrows.

"Enough for you?" asked Detective Villiers in a humorless way.

"No," I replied. "Maltcassion is being framed. I was with the dragon not two hours ago. This witness of yours wouldn't last ten minutes in a court of law. The same burden of proof is required for a dragon as it is for any other living creature."

"You're becoming something of a pest," returned Detective Villiers. "I've been a policeman for over twenty years. Who do you think did this if it wasn't Maltcassion?"

"Someone keen on getting the Dragonlands for themselves. King Snodd, perhaps, or Brecon. Both of them have an interest in the lands."

"You're crazy!" he said, pointing a finger at me.

"And what's more, you're dangerous. Accusing the king of complicity in murder? Have you any idea what could happen to you if I decided to make that public?" He glared at me, and I glared back.

"C'mon," he said finally. "There's another incident that I want you to see."

We drove in convoy the ten miles to Peterstow, where a field of cows had been torn limb from limb. It was not a pretty sight, and the flies were already buzzing happily in the heat.

"Seventy-two heifers," announced Villiers. "All dead. Talons, Miss Strange. Your friend Maltcassion. You have a duty to protect your charges and carry on your work as the Dragonslayer. Maltcassion has gone loco in his old age. You *must* defend the realm."

"He didn't do it."

Villiers rested his hand on my shoulder. His demeanor was less triumphant. Even he, I suspected, did not wholly believe what he was seeing. When you work for the king's law enforcement agencies, you can usually learn to spot a setup when you see it. And ignore it.

"It doesn't matter whether he did it or not, to be honest. All that matters is that there have been three separate incidents. You can check *The Dragonslayer's Manual* if you want."

I didn't need to. He was right. To counter a dragon's

deceit, three incidents with all the hallmarks of Drago-nattack were enough. That was the rule laid down by the Mighty Shandar four centuries ago and ratified by the Council of Dragons.

Perhaps it was my destiny to kill dragons. I was, after all, a Dragonslayer.

TWENTY-SEVEN

Sir Matt Grifflon

The crowds outside the Dragonstation had thinned
out by the time I arrived, probably because they were up
at the Dragonlands. The door to the Dragonstation was
open, and there was no sign of Gordon. Instead, sitting at
the kitchen table and reading through *The Dragonslayer's
Manual* was a striking man with a lantern jaw and long,
flowing blond hair. He looked up and smiled his best
smile as I entered, then rose politely to his feet. Sir Matt
Grifflon.

I felt a bit stupid; although I had good reason to
dislike and even fear him, my pulse was racing. I had all
his music, his poster was hidden in my closet, and to my

infinite shame, I was a member of his fan club. In a panic, I did the first thing I could think of: I pretended I didn't know who he was.

"Who are you?"

He looked shocked. "You're kidding, right?"

"No, I've absolutely no idea. Let me guess. You're here to do the drains?"

"Let me remind you," he muttered sharply, "I was in King Snodd's chambers when you visited."

"You're the footman? Sorry, didn't recognize you without the wig and pantaloons."

He scowled. "Let me give you a clue: ever heard the song 'A Horse, a Sword, and Me'?"

"You're a songwriter?"

"Okay, fun's over," he said, suddenly sensing my deliberate impertinence. "My name is . . . Sir Matt Grifflon." He said it in a dramatically deep voice that set the teacups rattling in the corner cupboard.

"His Gracious Majesty King Snodd IV," he continued in a businesslike tone, "has ordered me to personally oversee the dragon-killing process in order that this whole sorry business be brought to a successful conclusion as soon as possible. I have been given full rein over the manner in which it is done, and any order from me can be taken as from King Snodd himself."

He was sickeningly full of self-confidence.

"I'm sorry," I said. "What did you say your name was again?"

He glared at me. "I don't think you fully appreciate the seriousness of the situation. The rule of the Dragonpact is clear: three attacks, and the dragon must be destroyed. Proof is no longer a burden in this investigation, Miss Strange. If you do not have the stomach for the job, then step aside."

He was right, of course. As Villiers had pointed out, the rules were clear, and I was bound by them.

"I will do my duty!"

"And kill the dragon?"

"If that is what my duty entails."

"Not good enough," he said, his voice rising.

"No one can replace me unless I agree," I replied hotly.

"Will you kill the dragon? Yes or no?"

"*If* the dragon is rogue, I will do my duty!"

"*Yes or no!?*" He was shouting at me now, and I was shouting back.

"NO!" I yelled as hard as I could. The knight fell silent.

"I thought as much," said Grifflon in a normal tone. "King Snodd feels that you have been beguiled by the charm of the beast. Action must be taken to remove you from your post. You have failed in your fundamental duties as a Dragonslayer and as a loyal citizen of Hereford."

"Listen, Grifflon," I said, "why don't you do yourself a favor and head on home? The only way you get this job is over my dead body."

Grifflon was staring at me in a dangerous sort of way, and I suddenly felt as though my last sentence had probably *not* been the right thing to say.

"You force my hand in this, Miss Strange," murmured Grifflon, "by your stubborn refusal to kill the dragon. According to Old Magic from the days of Mu'shad Waseed, the first person to lay their hands on the hilt of Exhorbitus after the violent death of a Dragonslayer is, by Dragonpact decree, the next in line."

Sadly, this was true. Sir Matt Grifflon was smiling rather nastily at me and had taken a step closer. "Please," he said, pulling a small dagger from his pocket, "don't make this too hard on yourself. If you stand still, I can make it painless."

He was between me and the door, and I was just thinking of leaping out the window when a single word stopped Grifflon in his tracks. It was a simple word. Short, to the point, and unmistakable in its meaning. The word was *quark,* and the Quarkbeast said it.

"Quark," said the Quarkbeast again, positioning himself defiantly between me and Grifflon and revolving his five canines in a menacing fashion. My outrageously handsome would-be assassin looked at the Quarkbeast nervously.

"Call him off, Miss Strange."

"And let you kill me? Just how stupid do you think I am?"

"Quark," said the Quarkbeast, taking a step toward Griffon, who backed away.

"You can't hide behind a Quarkbeast forever, Miss Strange."

"It's Sunday tomorrow," I told him. "After the premonition of Maltcassion's death is proved wrong, I won't need to hide behind anything."

He glared at me, then ran out the door. The Quarkbeast sat on the rug and looked up at me with his large mauve eyes.

"You did good," I told him. "Thank you."

I looked out of the Dragonstation and into the street. Only a few die-hard Dragonslayer fans, some journalists, and Sir Matt's squires were in attendance, the latter doubtless to keep an eye on me in case I decided to make a run for it. I went back inside, locked the door, and caught the midmorning TV bulletin. King Snodd was giving a speech about how the Dragonlands were "historically part of Hereford" and said the whole kingdom had to act together to halt the perfidious Duke of Brecon from invading the country and threatening "all that we know and love."

I switched off the TV and went through to the kitchen where I found a note from Gordon van Gordon.

Dear Miss Strange,
I am sorry, but I have been called away to look after my mother, who has gout. I wish you the very best on this most difficult of days for you, and hope you will find the courage to act in the way that you think correct.
    Yours, Gordon van Gordon

"Coward," I muttered angrily, tearing up the paper and throwing it aside. I sat down to ponder my next move and still hadn't come up with a plan an hour later, when there was a loud hammering at the door. The Quarkbeast's hackles rose.

"Hello?" I yelled.

"Police" came the reply from outside.

"What do you want?"

"The Quarkbeast has been declared a dangerous animal," announced the impassive voice of the officer. "Harboring one is considered unlawful."

"Since when?"

"Since the king decreed it, seven minutes ago."

The rug was being pulled rapidly from under my feet.

"I need the Quarkbeast for protection," I answered a bit feebly.

"King Snodd has thought of that," bellowed the officer through the door. "His Majesty has sent Sir Matt Grifflon to guarantee your safety."

A shiver ran down my spine. "Grifflon wants to kill me so he can take over as Dragonslayer."

There was a pause. "You have been beguiled by the dragon, Miss Strange. Sir Matt tried to help you, and you set the Quarkbeast on him. King Snodd has given his word that no harm will come to you. There is no higher guarantee in the kingdom." He then added in a patronizing manner, "We don't want to hurt you or the Quarkbeast, Jennifer. All we want to do is *help* you."

I peeped cautiously out the window. The street had been blocked off, and three police cars were parked outside. There were about a dozen officers, and two of them were dressed in heavy armor. They had between them a riveted titanium box. A half-inch of titanium was about the only metal the Quarkbeast couldn't chew through. Standing to one side but still looking very much in charge of the operation was Sir Matt Grifflon.

"Please, Jennifer," said the officer, "open the door."

"Wait a minute," I said, running to the rear window. There were police out back, too. I was trapped.

"Either you surrender the Quarkbeast, or we take it and arrest you for noncompliance with a royal decree," said the officer as I returned to the front door. "If the Quarkbeast so much as looks at us in a funny way, we will have no choice but to destroy it. The choice is yours. I'll give you a minute to decide."

I looked down at the Quarkbeast. "It's fourteen against two, chum. What do you say?"

"Quark."

"I thought you'd say that. But I'm not risking your life for mine. Let's find another way out."

I ran to the Rolls-Royce and unclipped Exhorbitus. As the Quarkbeast watched me with growing interest, I attacked the wall. The sword cut deep into the brickwork, slicing through the masonry as though it were wet paper. Three quick slashes, and we were through to the property next door.

"Sorry!" I said to the surprised resident, who had been watching *The Snodd v. Brecon War Show Live* when his wall came down and a Dragonslayer and her Quarkbeast jumped through.

We didn't stop there. Holding the sword in front of me, I ran across the room and went through the next wall and into a coin-operated laundromat. Water sprayed everywhere as the sword sliced easily through the washing machines. We heard an explosion, which must have been the police blowing down the door of the Dragonstation, but by that time we had cut our way out of the laundromat and into the house beyond that. Luckily this one was empty, and the next wall brought us out into the daylight at the end of the row.

Exhorbitus was too unwieldy to allow me to run far, and I wasn't going to use the sword on anyone anyway, so I hid it beneath some rubbish in an empty building site and ran into the network of small alleyways in the old town behind the cathedral. As the yells of the police grew louder behind us, I stopped. We couldn't run forever, my Volkswagen was in the other direction, and the safety of Dragonlands was almost twenty miles away.

I turned to the Quarkbeast and told him to run off and hide. He looked all doleful and made signs that his place was by me, so I had to be stern and explain that this wasn't the time for a final stand that would surely leave us both dead, and that given a choice, the police would follow me rather than him. He seemed to understand my every word and lolloped off.

I waited until Sir Matt and the officers could see me from the far end of the street, then darted off in the opposite direction. I ran through the narrow streets with Grifflon and the police barely a hundred yards away. I turned left, then right, then found myself outside

Zambini Towers. I was out of breath, luck, and ideas, and before I knew what I was doing, I darted inside and locked the bolt.

I hoped that Wizard Moobin might have returned from the border of the Dragonlands and would help me, but as soon as I entered, I could tell that the old hotel was empty. For the first time ever, I noticed an eerie silence within the echoing corridors. There was no hum, no static, no strangeness, nothing. All the sorcerers—even the mad ones from the eleventh floor—must have been up at the Dragonlands to assist with Big Magic, in whatever form it might take. I was entirely on my own.

I dashed through the open doors of the Palm Court, looking for a place to hide, but then my heart fell. Next to the fountain was Lady Mawgon, sitting bolt upright in a dining room chair with her hands on her lap. She was dressed in blacker-than-usual crinolines, gloves, and a veil.

"Good afternoon, Lady Mawgon."

"I've been waiting for you, Jennifer."

"Listen," I said, "I know we've not been getting along very well, but there's Big Magic going on tomorrow at noon, and I've got to be there."

I was interrupted by a sharp report from the front door as the lock was shot off, followed by a cry from Sir Matt. There were footfalls on the steps, and I heard shouts and cries in the lobby. There was no place to hide except behind the central fountain. I'd be unseen from the door, but even a cursory search of the Palm Court would uncover me.

"Sir Matt?" called out Lady Mawgon. "Would you come into the Palm Court, please?"

Sir Matt stepped in and nodded respectfully to Lady Mawgon. "My lady," he said, "you have her?"

There was one of those long pauses that seem to go on forever. I closed my eyes.

"I have not seen the wretched child all afternoon," Lady Mawgon announced. "When you are finished with her, you may send her to me."

"Don't think me untrusting," said Sir Matt, and he beckoned his officers to search the Palm Court. As he stepped forward, Lady Mawgon placed her hand lightly on my shoulder. They could not have missed me, but they did—and I breathed a sigh of relief. Lady Mawgon had occluded me from sight. It's not the same as invisibility, which has eluded even the finest magicians for centuries, but the spell would keep me from being easily noticed—exploiting the same phenomenon that keeps you from seeing your car keys when they are sitting on the desk in front of you. To make it work, I stayed perfectly still and made no noise.

"Nothing in here, sir," said an officer, and trotted out to search the rest of the building.

"She won't get far," replied Grifflon. "The whole of

the Old Town is sealed off." He turned back to Lady Mawgon and lowered his voice. "If I find out you've hidden her, I will return—and my revenge will be frightful."

She gave him one of her most imperious looks, and Sir Matt called off the search. The wizards, ever worried about thieves, had left frighteners in their rooms, and even the burliest officers were quaking with fear at what they had seen. Within five minutes they had gone, and Lady Mawgon took her hand off my shoulder.

"There is Big Magic to be completed," she said in a quiet voice and without looking me in the eye, "and it behooves me to set our differences aside. Stay here tonight and get a good night's sleep. I will watch over you."

I wanted to give her a hug but decided against it. "Thank you, Lady Mawgon, I—"

"It is my duty," she said. "Nothing more."

I went to find Tiger.

TWENTY-EIGHT

Escape from Zambini Towers

Lady Mawgon was true to her word and sat up all night in the lobby. Tiger and I talked until late down in the kitchens. At one o'clock A.M., a thump in the laundry room made us nervous until we found that it was the Quarkbeast, who had managed to sneak back into Zambini Towers without being noticed.

The early-morning radio bulletins estimated that the crowds up at the Dragonlands now topped eight million people, and anticipation was high. Neither King Snodd nor Sir Matt Grifflon had made any further proclamations, so I could only assume that they were still looking for me. Unstable Mabel made Tiger and me pancakes for breakfast, and then made a special batch for the Quark-beast, who liked them with curry powder instead of flour.

"Every exit of the building is covered by at least three Imperial Guards," said Tiger, who had gone around to check. This was not good news.

"I need to retrieve Exhorbitus from its hiding place and then get to the Dragonstation," I replied. "No one is permitted to hinder a Dragonslayer while on official duties, and to be honest, once I'm in the armored Rolls-Royce, nothing but an artillery shell could stop me. And even King Snodd would think twice before trying to kill me in broad daylight and in front of the TV cameras."

"It's five hundred yards to the Dragonstation," said Tiger. "They're not after me. Perhaps I could get the Slayermobile for you?"

"Can you drive?"

"How hard can it be?"

"Quite hard. The Slayermobile is like driving the heaviest car ever—and from inside a mailbox."

Just then Lady Mawgon walked into the kitchens and handed me a copy of the *Daily Mollusc*. The front page had banner headlines explaining how everything was fine after all, so it was no longer necessary for me to slay Maltcassion. It added that the Duke of Brecon and King Snodd had kissed and made up, the Quarkbeast was no longer an illegal animal, the sale of marzipan was banned, and all foundlings everywhere were to be reunited with their parents.

"This is all far too good to be true," I muttered, and as soon as I had, the enchantment crumbled. I was no longer reading a newspaper but simply staring at a colorless gray pebble.

"What you have in your hand is a Pollyanna Stone," Lady Mawgon told me. "Whoever holds the pebble will see what they expect or hope to see. It might be of use if you are stopped on the way." She turned away, paused, then turned back.

"If you tell *anyone* I've been nice to you," she said, narrowing her eyes, "I will make it my solemn duty to make both your lives as unbearable as possible. And don't think I'm not going to have you both replaced on Monday, for I will." And without another word, she left the room.

"The sorcerers are an odd bunch, aren't they?" said Tiger with a smile.

"They grow on you," I replied, "even Lady Mawgon-Gorgon there."

"I heard that!" came a voice from the corridor.

We finished breakfast and talked about a plan for me to get to the Dragonstation. None passed the stringent "remotely plausible" test. We were still scratching our heads when we heard a noise outside the kitchen and found that the Quarkbeast had dragged a baby stroller from one of the building's many storage rooms. He looked at us excitedly and wagged his tail.

"Brilliant!" said Tiger. "The Quarkbeast's a genius! Listen carefully: We'll need some baby clothes, a piece of cardboard, a felt-tip pen, some old clothes, and a wig."

Twenty minutes later and after Tiger had wished me the very best of luck, I slipped out of the garage doors at the back of Zambini Towers and walked toward the guards on the corner. Dressed in one of the Sisters Karamazov's old outfits and a red wig I had borrowed from Mr. Zambini's costume box, I was pushing the Quarkbeast in the stroller. The Quarkbeast was wrapped up in a baby shawl and wearing a pretty pink bonnet. A sign tied to the front of the stroller announced that I was collecting for the Troll War Widows Fund.

I wasn't convinced this would work, but Tiger was smart, and it was the only idea we had. "Everyone has lost someone in the Troll Wars," he had explained. "So no one will stop you."

He was right. Since Troll War widows begging for coins were not at all uncommon, I was ignored by the members of the Imperial Guard, who were searching every car on the roads. There were posters of me up on the walls, telling the general public how I was a dangerous lunatic and a traitor and had to be stopped as a matter of national security. As I crossed the road, a police car passed with a large loudspeaker blaring from the roof, offering an earldom and a guest spot on the *You Bet Your Life!* quiz show to whoever turned me in.

I quickened my pace and made it to where I had hid Exhorbitus. I wrapped the sword in a blanket, placed it under the stroller, and turned into the road where the Dragonstation was located.

There was POLICE LINE DO NOT CROSS tape barring my way. Outside the Dragonstation were two Imperial Guard armored cars and at least a dozen soldiers, all armed. I took a deep breath and walked toward them. It was all going well; if I could make it by and then sneak inside to the Rolls-Royce all would be—

"Quark."

"Shhh."

"Good morning, ma'am. Going somewhere?" Two of the Imperial Guards had walked across to see me. It was galling. I was almost within spitting distance of the Dragonstation.

"Spare a groat for a poor Troll War widow?"

"This road's closed," announced the first soldier sharply. He didn't look as though he had a very charitable nature. "What are you doing here?"

"Taking my poor, sweet, fatherless, and ill child to

his checkup. He has bad calluses on his legs, a bald patch, and his poor orphaned heart, well, it's—"

"I get the point. Identification papers?"

I handed him the Pollyanna Stone. If he thought I was a war widow, then all would be well. If he was expecting the worst or was even vaguely suspicious, all would be lost. I was lucky. The guard looked at the pebble as though it really *were* identification papers, turned it over, and said, "Name?"

"Mrs. Jennifer Jones."

"Identification number?"

"86231524."

He nodded and passed the pebble back to me. "Okay, move along."

I thanked him and started to walk off.

"Wait!" said the second soldier, and I held my breath. He dug into his pocket and pulled out a coin. "Here's a groat for you. I fought in the Troll Wars and lost some good friends. May I see the baby?" Before I could say or do anything, he looked into the stroller at the Quarkbeast. The Quarkbeast stared up at him.

"What's his name?"

"Quark?" said the Quarkbeast, blinking nervously.

"Sweet kid. Okay, Mrs. Jones, move along." I walked on, my heart beating heavily and a cold sweat on my forehead.

"Well," I heard the soldier whisper to his colleague,

"I've seen some ugly babies in my time, but that little Quark Jones is uglier than all of them put together."

The guards turned away, and as soon as I was opposite the broken-in front door of the Dragonstation, I jumped inside and ran to the Rolls-Royce, the Quarkbeast close behind. I loaded the lance and Exhorbitus and jumped into the driver's seat. The Slayermobile whispered into life; I engaged first gear and floored the accelerator.

With a splintering of wood, I drove through the locked garage doors and pushed the Imperial Guard's armored car out of the way. I pulled the steering wheel over and sped up the street, the *spang* of rifle fire bouncing off the heavy iron plating. At the end of the street was a barricade of cars, manned by a group of policemen whose puny weapons could not hope to damage the Slayermobile. They jumped out of the way as the vehicle tore through their cars, the sharp spikes ripping the bodywork as though it were tissue paper.

Once I was out of the tight police cordon that ringed the Old Town, I found quite a different scene awaiting me. The public, who had been told that a Dragonslayer—although not necessarily me—would be heading up to the Dragonlands that morning, had lined the route in eager expectation. An excited yell went up as the Slayermobile appeared, and several hundred flags waved in unison. Somewhere a brass band started up, and garlands of flowers were thrown in the path of the Rolls-Royce.

Sir Matt Grifflon had set all this up for himself. He had thought, in his arrogance, that I would have been caught and dispatched before that morning.

I slowed down as the danger subsided. There was little that Grifflon or even King Snodd would dare to try with all these potential witnesses. As I drove past, the crowds broke ranks and followed the Slayermobile in one long procession. We were joined by the guild of master builders, two marching bands, and a contingent from the Troll Wars Veterans Association. TV cameras at every corner beamed my progress live to half a billion viewers worldwide. From China to Patagonia and from Hawaii to Vietnam, my progress was eagerly watched.

TWENTY-NINE

Back to the Dragonlands

My journey unimpeded, I arrived at the Dragonlands and drove slowly through the parting crowd. I felt the slight fizz as I passed through the marker stones, and then stopped the car. Safe at last, I climbed out of the Slayermobile as the news crews came as close to the boundary markers as they dared.

First on the scene was a SnoddNews film crew. The reporter, jostled from behind, made a short introduction to what would turn out to be the biggest news scoop of her career.

"I am speaking live from the Kingdom of Hereford, where we are about to witness the last round of a titanic struggle that began four hundred years ago with the

Dragonpact, and finishes at twelve o'clock noon here high on a hill just outside the Kingdom of Hereford. A struggle that will finally see the Mighty Shandar complete his work to rid the kingdoms of dragons once and for all." She pointed the microphone at me. "A few words? We're live."

"My name is Jennifer Strange," I began. "I am the Last Dragonslayer. I have grave doubts about the claims of the supposed crimes, but by the laws of the Dragonpact, I am not permitted to refuse my duty. I hope that one day you will all forgive me, although I know I shall never be able to afford myself the same privilege."

The press clamored for more, but I ignored them. I caught a glimpse of Sir Matt Grifflon staring at me with daggers in his eyes. He was standing next to a couple of Berzerkers, who were hitting each other with bricks in readiness for the battle. I gave them all a wan smile and drove away from the baying crowd.

Once out of their sight, I stopped the Rolls-Royce and climbed out. It was barely eleven o'clock; I had time to catch my breath.

"You're back," said a voice.

I didn't even bother turning around. "Hello, Shandar," I replied.

He was sitting on a rock. "You must *not* kill the dragon," he said quite simply. "I *order* you not to kill the dragon. You will regret it. The Dragonpact will be destroyed. The dragons will be free to once again roam the land, killing and plundering, and the Ununited Kingdoms will collapse into a new dark age more evil and sinister than you can imagine. Humans, made slaves, will be ruled by the dragons, whose hearts are as black as the deepest cavern, their one wish the destruction of the human race."

"Is this another recording?"

"I have placed this recording here as a warning against anyone trying to kill the last dragon. Believe nothing that it says to you. It can lie in thought, deed, and gesture. I repeat: Return now and leave the dragon alone."

I was confused. "But by the terms of your decree, the dragon is rogue and must be destroyed!" The image twitched and went back to the beginning.

"You must *not* kill the dragon," he said quite simply. "I *order* you not to kill the dragon . . ."

I watched the speech again, but the magic was old and weak, so before I had heard the message three times, Shandar was merely a voice on the wind. Naturally I agreed with him but was suspicious of his command *not* to kill the last dragon, when he had been paid twenty dray-weights of gold to do precisely that. Had I been beguiled by the dragon? Did Shandar have another agenda? Was I smart enough to see through the possible lies? Thoroughly confused, I set off into the Dragonlands.

I drove up a hill, followed the ridge for a little way, and then descended into a beech forest. I had to steer the large Rolls-Royce very carefully between tree stumps and fallen branches. Twice I had to back up and try a new way through, but soon the forest thinned out and I found myself looking onto a large, flat meadow next to a stream. I drove across the short grass as grazing sheep moved lazily out of my way, then crested a low rise and stopped, not believing what I saw.

I turned off the engine and stepped out onto the springy turf. Across the low valley was a sea of white tape that crisscrossed the untouched land, tied to pegs hammered into the ground. Someone was in the Dragonlands. Someone was already staking claims.

I heard a cheery whistling on the breeze and turned to see a small man in a brown suit and an unmistakable derby hat. I stared for a moment, not quite believing what I was seeing. He had *lied* to me. He wasn't valiant or trustworthy—and it didn't seem as though he was looking after his mother, either. I cursed myself for my stupidity, for I had made this all possible—only a Dragonslayer or an apprentice may enter the Dragonlands. Gordon van Gordon was cheerfully banging claim stakes into the ground and hadn't noticed I was watching him.

"I trusted you, Gordon."

He jumped as I spoke and looked up at me but didn't seem too worried.

"Trust is a trait you should be proud of, Jennifer—and I'm very glad you're so pleasant. If you'd been obnoxious, this would have been ten times as hard."

"Let me see."

He approached and gave me one of the stakes. There was an aluminum disk attached, and it was stamped with the name of the company Mr. Trimble had been negotiating for: The Consolidated Useful Stuff Land Development Corporation. Gordon had successfully claimed the land. The area enclosed within the stakes legally belonged to ConStuff—or would, as soon as the dragon was dead and the marker stones lost their power. And Gordon had claimed a *lot*. There were marker tapes tied to stakes as far as I could see.

I shook my head sadly. "Why did you do it, Gordon?"

"Business, Miss Strange—nothing personal. You have many fine qualities that I admire. You should have been born a century ago, when values such as yours meant something." Gordon smiled, but it was a smile I hadn't seen before. The Gordon I knew, the friendly and helpful Dragonslayer's apprentice, had never been real at all.

"You had me fooled."

"Don't beat yourself up over it," he said kindly. "We've been running the Last Dragonslayer drill for a number of years now."

I frowned. "This was all *planned?*"

He knocked a peg in, wrapped a tape around it, and

walked off in the direction of a stream. I followed, more out of shocked disbelief than anything else.

"We knew that Brian Spalding was expecting someone to replace him. He resisted all our attempts to get him to appoint our own apprentice, so we watched him, waiting for the time the new Dragonslayer would come and take his place. It just so happened that you chanced along on my shift."

"How long were you waiting?"

"Sixty-eight years. A team of six people around the clock. My father gave his working life to ConStuff. He watched Brian Spalding for over thirty years."

"Thirty years? Just for some real estate?"

"You don't get it, do you?" Gordon said as though I were some sort of idiot. "King Snodd and the Duke of Brecon are powerful, Miss Strange. They have the power, as you have seen, to change the law at a whim and outlaw their citizens at their command. But even they are powerless when it comes to the might of commerce. Governments may come and go; wars will reshape the Ununited Kingdoms many times. But companies will stay and flourish. Show me any major event on this planet, and I will show you the economic reason behind it. Commerce is all powerful, Miss Strange. Commerce rules our lives. ConStuff has put a lot of time and expense into Project Dragon, and their investment is about to bear fruit." He spread his arms wide and looked around. "Do you have any idea just how much this parcel of land is worth?"

"Of course," I replied. "I have a very good idea of the value of the Dragonlands. But you and I are talking about different currencies. You're talking about gold and silver, cash and securities. I'm talking about the sheer beauty of the land, the value of unpolluted parkland made wild and staying wild forever."

"Dream on, Strange," Gordon sneered. "In every direction are hundreds of thousands of greedy speculators eager to lay claim to a few square yards. While you have been gallivanting around pondering the imponderables, I have laid claim to sixty percent of the lands. We already have plans drawn up. We will build an access road through that oak forest, and just over there"—he indicated a small copse of silver birches—"will be a retail park for over seventy shops, with parking for a thousand cars. Over there"—he pointed to a hill in the other direction—"will be a luxury housing development. Just beyond that hill there will be a power station and marzipan refinery. This is progress, Miss Strange. A billion moolah worth of progress. We were lucky you turned out to have such high ideals. If you had fallen for King Snodd's scheme to claim the Dragonlands on his behalf, you might have been something of a nuisance to us. As it is, everything has turned out admirably."

"Then I pity you," I replied. "I pity you because you will never know or see a decent act. You have given nothing, you will receive nothing."

"I have a bank balance that proves you wrong, Jennifer. My share alone in this project amounts to over thirty million. I watched Brian Spalding doggedly for over twenty-three years. Don't tell me I don't deserve it!"

We stared at each other for a moment.

"So all those Dragonattacks. They were arranged by ConStuff?"

"Certainly. As soon as the prophecy began, we knew we could use it to our advantage. Even King Snodd and the Duke of Brecon wouldn't have dared fake a Dragonattack. We just helped things along. Massaged fate, if you like. Look at it our way, and we have actually *helped* solve the Dragon Problem. I think the Mighty Shandar would actually be grateful."

"And the prophecy that began all this? You as well?"

"If only!" said Gordon, laughing. "If *that* were in our power, we could have engineered all this sixty-eight years ago. Nope, that wasn't us."

ConStuff and Gordon were playing with things quite outside their understanding. "Money is a form of alchemy," Mother Zenobia had told me. "It turns kind, normal people into greed-mongers, intent only on acquisitiveness."

"You have no idea what's going on, do you?" I told him, my voice rising. "I know that, because *I* have no idea what's going on, and I'm the Dragonslayer. Everyone wants the dragon dead except me and Shandar. Even the dragon wants the dragon dead. If I were you, I'd get out of the Dragonlands while you still can."

"You're blabbering, Jennifer. I'll be staking claims until the first Berzerker comes over that hill."

I couldn't think of what to do, so I pulled up a marker stake and threw it into the stream. Gordon wasn't impressed. He pulled a revolver out of his waistband and pointed it at me.

"Be a good little girl and leave me alone. Do something useful like kill the dragon so we can finish this all up and get to the part where I get handed wads of—"

There was a growling and a snapping. The Quarkbeast had left the safety of the Rolls-Royce and was running down the hill as fast as his short legs could carry him. Out in the Dragonlands, his instincts were taking over, and he was going to protect me whether I liked it or not.

"Call him off, Miss Strange. I'll shoot him, I swear I will!"

I wasn't keen on Gordon, but no one deserves to be savaged by a Quarkbeast.

"Stop!" I shouted to the Quarkbeast. "Danger!"

But he kept on coming, his jaws rattling dangerously, his sharp obsidian teeth glinting unkindly in the
sunlight. There was a shot, and the Quarkbeast fell,
rolled over twice in the heather, and lay still. I looked
across at Gordon, who now turned the smoking pistol
back to me.

"Don't even think about it!" he said angrily. "I never
liked the little tyke anyway. Run along and do your duty,
or by King Snodd and St. Grunk, I'll shoot you where
you stand and get Sir Matt Grifflon in here to do your
work for you!"

I tried to find something to say, but nothing came
out.

"Well!" sneered Gordon. "Quite the Dragonslayer,
aren't you? I was wondering how you could possibly
have handled this any worse. All you had to do was kill
a dragon, and instead we've got a major war about to
break out. Destiny is unkind sometimes, isn't it? How
many deaths will you have on your conscience? A thousand? Two thousand? How much are your fancy scruples
worth now?"

"Stop!" I shouted angrily.

"Stop?" he repeated with a triumphant smile. "Or
what? What will you do?"

I suddenly knew *exactly* what I'd do. "Or I'll fire you,
Gordon."

"Well, you can't," he sneered. "I resign."

"You resign?"

"Yes, I— "

"You mean you're *not* my apprentice?"

He clapped his hand over his mouth, and his face drained of color.

"No!" he yelled, throwing the gun away and changing his voice to a mournful plea. "I don't resign! I'm sorry, *please* take me on again, I don't want to end like— "

There was a bright flash and a smell of burned paper as Gordon was reduced to little more than the powder you might find in a Cup-a-Soup. Only his suit, derby hat, and a smoking revolver remained to show that he had ever been. None but a Dragonslayer or an apprentice could enter the Dragonlands.

I walked over to where the Quarkbeast was lying still in the heather. I dropped to my knees and rested my hand gently on his forehead. His large eyes were closed; he almost looked asleep. A legend about Quarkbeasts says they are sent by the spirits of dead relatives to watch over you in times of uncertainty. My father had sent the Quarkbeast, I was sure of it. The small animal, although repulsive to many and possessed of disgusting personal habits and, yes, a bit smelly, had done his duty without regard for his own safety.

I moved his body to a hillock above a bend in the

stream and placed a pile of stones over his small form. I topped this with a larger rock upon which I scratched the word *Quark* and the date. In the warm summer sunshine, I stood for a moment. He had been a good, loyal friend, and he had given his life to save me.

THIRTY

Noon

I returned to the Slayermobile and drove to Malt-cassion's lair in the clearing in the forest. I parked and stepped out, noticing that the large marker stone was humming louder than usual. The dragon was sitting up on his hind legs. He was far taller than I had guessed — at least the height of one of Hereford's landships. He sniffed the air and listened carefully with his finely tuned ears.

"I am sorry about your small friend," he said, looking down at me. "He had a good soul, despite his appalling table manners."

I thanked him, and he told me he'd known I would come, despite my misgivings.

"The Mighty Shandar just spoke to me," I said. "He demanded that you were to be spared. How do you account for that?"

Maltcassion growled angrily. "Don't you dare speak of that scoundrel in my presence!"

I was shocked. "Scoundrel? You mean Shandar?"

Maltcassion roared; a sheet of flame burst from his throat and shot across the clearing, where it ignited a Douglas fir. The tree went up like a Roman candle. I took a few hasty steps back from the heat.

"I told you not to mention his name!"

"I don't understand!" I yelled above the crackling of the burning tree. He beckoned me to move away, and I joined him.

"Why do you think you are the first Dragonslayer to ever come up to the Dragonlands?"

"I don't know."

"Then let me ask you something else. Why do you suppose you are here at all?"

I thought the question a bit obvious. "To slay any dragons guilty of violating the Dragonpact?"

"But in four centuries none of us has *ever* violated the pact. Have you any idea why?"

"Because you respect the Dragonpact?"

"No. I'll tell you. Shandar suggested the use of a force field surrounding the marker stones to keep humans out. Such an act of magic is vast. He requested that we help him, and we readily agreed, binding the magic of the marker stones so tightly it could never be undone except by the death of the dragon it was there to protect."

"And?"

"He tricked us. The weave of the magic was tighter than we imagined. The marker stones don't just keep humans out, *but us in.* These Dragonlands are not a safe haven but a prison!"

I digested this new information. "Then the Dragonpact wasn't a pact at all!"

"Exactly. Shandar earned his twenty dray-weights of gold, believe me. The first dragon who tried to get out was vaporized instantly. We sent around a message of the danger, and here we have sat, dwindling in numbers, communicating rarely, and watching our magic slowly siphoned out of us by the energy of the very force field that was meant to protect us!"

"So why have Dragonslayers at all?"

"Window dressing," replied the dragon. "The Dragonslayers, far from being a most noble profession, are really nothing more than a contractual obligation. In Shandar's plan, you would never have come up here at all."

"Then . . . I don't have to kill you."

The dragon raised a claw into the air and wagged it at me.

"Well, that's the *wrong* answer, I'm afraid," he said reproachfully. "We've planned this for a long time. You were chosen by us to do this deed; at midday you *have* to kill me!"

I could feel tears well up. It was all so unfair. "But I've never killed anything in my life!"

"Big Magic is by definition highly specific. Someone like you *must* do it."

"What's special about me? Why can't Sir Matt Grifflon do it?"

"You are more special than you realize, Jennifer."

I stared up at the old dragon, hearing an echo of what Mother Zenobia had told me. Something astonishing was going to happen, and I was a part of it.

"I'm ready," I said in a quiet voice. "Tell me what is expected of me."

The dragon fixed me with his jewellike eyes. "You already know what is expected of you, Jennifer. I wish I had the answers, but I don't. I am only the last in a long line of greater minds. All I know is that you have to discharge your duty using your own free will and judgment. This is your moment. You will do the right thing."

I fetched Exhorbitus from the Slayermobile as a clock started to strike twelve somewhere in the far distance, and Maltcassion lifted his chin to reveal the soft flesh beneath his throat. I started to cry; large salty drops ran down my face and onto the soft earth. Sometimes your destiny takes you to dark places where you'd rather not be, but destiny, as they say, is destiny.

I held the sword aloft as a light wind whipped the leaves and twigs into motion. I placed the tip against the dragon's skin and paused.

"Goodbye, Jennifer. *Gwanjii*. I forgive you," he said.

I closed my eyes and thrust the sword upward as hard as I could. The effect was immediate and dramatic. Maltcassion shuddered and slumped to the ground with a mighty crash. A large cloud of dust was thrown up by his falling bulk, and I was knocked backward into the dirt. Winded, I struggled to my feet, expecting some sort of magic to start happening. I stole a glance at Maltcassion, then hurriedly looked away. The jewel in his forehead had stopped glowing, and an unnerving silence invaded the forest.

Abruptly, the marker stone in the center of his lair stopped humming. What if I had been wrong? Big Magic, Wizard Moobin had told me, has rarely more than a twenty percent success rate. I had trusted Maltcassion and done what he had asked, but there was no magic. No high winds, no noises, no mysterious flashes of light — nothing. If this was Big Magic, it was a grave disappointment.

I suddenly felt very small and solitary. One person

alone in three hundred and twenty square miles of disputed territory, sandwiched between two huge armies with artillery and landships, and with only forty tons of dead dragon for company. I apologized to the large beast, but it was over.

The ancient order of the dragons was dead.

THIRTY-ONE

Anger

I looked around at the forest, wondering what to do. Far in the distance was the rumble of artillery. A few seconds later a faint whistle preceded a shell that exploded somewhere in the Dragonlands. The war had begun.

Everything that had happened over the past few days now seemed unimportant. I had failed Wizard Moobin and the Big Magic; I had failed Maltcassion and the centuries-dead Dragon Council. Maltcassion had suggested I'd been chosen for this task, but I was obviously not good enough. I had felt no remorse when Gordon van Gordon was vaporized, and I felt nothing but disgust for ConStuff, King Snodd, and the hordes of claimants who waited eagerly outside the Dragonlands. I had once pulled the convent cat's tail, too. Perhaps there had been a mistake; there was *another* Jennifer Strange somewhere, one with true purity and goodness. Perhaps she would have triumphed.

There was another distant *boom* and a second artillery shell came whistling over and exploded, opening up a hole in the fertile earth of the Dragonlands. The old dragon looked more like a huge pile of rubble than ever. Perhaps in years to come, someone would remember what had happened here and open a small museum that explained what the Dragonlands had been like, the treachery of the Mighty Shandar, and the final effort of the dragons to survive. On the other hand, perhaps they wouldn't bother. They'd probably build a museum to Yogi Baird—and it would be sponsored by Yummy Flakes breakfast cereal.

I sat on the trunk of a fallen tree and listened as another shell was lobbed into the lands. Only a few more minutes, and the battle would really begin. King Snodd's massive landships would lumber across the hills, churning up the ground with their heavy tracks, laying waste as they pushed their way toward the Duchy of Brecon and beyond in their campaign to conquer Wales. I ducked instinctively as a shell landed in the forest about a hundred yards away and felled an old Douglas fir that crashed into the undergrowth. The aim was wild and erratic; the Hereford gunners were firing blindly into the Dragonlands.

My pulse started to race, and a bad feeling rose within me like a fever. As a red veil of rage descended, I tried to swallow the anger down, but it was too strong. I simmered for a few seconds; then I boiled. All rational thought vanished. The image of the Quarkbeast and the leering face of Gordon assaulted me.

I thought of the crowds around the Dragonlands, waiting for the moment of the dragon's death with greedy expectation. I wanted to run to the marker stones and attack and kill and maim as many greedy, bloodsucking, dragon-hating people as I could.

I leaped for Exhorbitus and grasped the hilt with a tightness that made me cry out in pain. I felt strong enough to take on a landship, to tear at its iron hull with my bare hands and face the guns with an iron resolve. I let fly at a boulder with the sword, hoping to release the rage; the boulder fell neatly in two, but I felt more angry, not less. A noise like a hurricane had started in my head, and every muscle in my body tightened like a spring.

Then the pain started. A burning sensation attacked every nerve ending in my body. Instinctively, I opened my mouth and screamed. It was quite a scream. They heard it at the marker stones. They heard it in Hereford. But it wasn't just a scream. It was a pointer, a marker, a conduit for other energy to follow, like the spark that precedes a lightning bolt.

I pointed the blade of Exhorbitus at Maltcassion, and

from the blued steel flowed a sinuous white source of energy that moved into the old dragon's body and made the lifeless husk squirm and dance. I kept screaming, the noise dominating everything. The dust lifted from the ground, and the water in the river began to steam. The trees shed their leaves and birds dropped from the sky. I saw more shells falling to earth in a slow and lazy arc, but I could not hear them. One of them exploded nearby, and I felt a piece of shrapnel pluck at my sleeve. A tree fell in the clearing, but I didn't flinch. All that mattered was the uncontrolled rage that wrung the energy from the air. The sky darkened, and a bolt of lightning descended to the marker stone, splitting it in two.

Darkness opened in front of me as I released the last of the air from my lungs. I knew then that this had been a scream of dragons long dead. It was a scream of renewal. It was Big Magic.

THIRTY-TWO

The New Order

"I s it dead?" said a voice.

"Not it, *she*," said another.

"I can never tell the difference. Is *she* dead, then?"

"I hope not."

I opened my eyes and found myself staring into the kindly faces of not one but *two* dragons. They were not much different from Maltcassion, except they were smaller and looked a great deal younger. My temper had left me; all I was left with was an aching body and throbbing temples.

"Do either of you have an aspirin?" I croaked, my throat feeling as though I had slept with a toad in my mouth.

The dragon who had spoken first gave a sort of

hurumphing cough that I took to be a snigger. "We're glad you still have your sense of humor."

I sat up. "My sense of humor I kept," I replied, clutching my head and groaning. "What I lost was Maltcassion, the Quarkbeast, the Dragonlands, and most of free Wales."

"You could do with a drink," said the second dragon. He nodded, and a glass of water appeared beside me.

"How did you do that?" I asked.

"Magic," replied the dragon.

I smiled and sipped at it gratefully.

"Hmm." One of the dragons unfurled his wings and looked at them thoughtfully, the way a baby might examine its own foot and wonder what it was for.

"Two of you?" I asked. "Two from one? Is that how it works?"

"Usually," replied the second dragon. He sneezed violently, and a small jet of flame leaped across the clearing and ignited a shrub.

"Whoops," he said. "I'm going to have to get *that* under control."

The dragons sniffed around, eager to investigate their new world. Of Maltcassion there was no sign, just a jewel on top of a pile of gray ash that was being blown by a light wind into the Dragonlands.

"Shh!" I said. "Listen!"

They both cocked an ear into the breeze and frowned. "We don't hear anything."

"That's exactly it!" I replied. "The guns. They've *stopped*."

"Of course," countered the dragon. "The Old Magic is unwoven. New Magic has taken its place. The force field is back up, but we may pass freely in both directions. The Dragonlands are still Dragonlands. Oh, but I have no manners. Allow me to introduce myself. My name is Feldspar Axiom Firebreath IV, and this is Colin."

Colin the dragon bowed solemnly and said, "We would like to thank you, Miss Strange, for without your fortitude and adherence to duty, dear Maltcassion really *would* have been the last dragon."

I tried to make sense of this strange course of events. "I wasn't chosen for my purity, was I?"

"I'm afraid not," replied Feldspar. "But don't be disappointed. It's just as well that true virtue is rare, for it would have to be balanced by the purest evil. The Dragon Council chose well. I would never have guessed in a million years that you were a Berzerker."

I stared at them each in turn.

"A Berzerker? Me?"

"Of course. Didn't you know?"

I thought I had always been in control of my temper, but perhaps I'd been holding back long-forgotten childhood tantrums. Maybe Mother Zenobia knew more about me than she had ever revealed. Now that I knew, of course, I would have to be careful. I was a member of a rare class of fearless warriors, a person who could draw energy from those around them during uncontrollable bouts of rage and channel it with terrifying violence against a foe. Even rarer, I was a Berzerker who could *contain* her temper. Most couldn't. If I let it be known, I would almost certainly be the subject of relentless study. I shuddered at the prospect.

"You won't tell anyone?"

"You would be surprised how many concealed Berzerkers walk among the citizenry. You have a gift. Learn to use it wisely."

"So you planned all this?"

"It was a grand plan, Jennifer, four hundred years in the making. When Shandar imprisoned us, we knew that as individuals we could do nothing to unweave the strong magic. Dragons have always been renewed by death. Kill one, and two rise in its place. Mu'shad Waseed didn't know that, but Shandar did. That's why he didn't want you to kill Maltcassion. A dragon that dies of old age leaves no offspring."

"So anytime in the past four hundred years a Dragonslayer could have killed a dragon and added one more to the population?"

"It wouldn't have done much good. Two dragons imprisoned instead of one? No; we needed to do more. We needed a spell to overcome all that Shandar had done and a little bit more besides. A spell of almost incalculable size and complexity. A spell that could release us and recharge the power of wizardry, lest Shandar returns to make good his promise to destroy the dragons. He is an evil man, but an honorable one. Twenty dray-weights of gold is a sizable chunk of change, and I'm not sure he's the sort of wizard who likes giving refunds."

"Big Magic."

"*Precisely*. But Big Magic is unpredictable stuff, and we were still without the vast quantity of raw wizidrical energy we needed to make it work. Shandar cast the spell, so we would need *more* than the power of Shandar to undo it. Such power is spread too thinly upon this planet to be useful — we needed to find a way to collect it."

"Like the grains of gold on the beach," I murmured, remembering Mother Zenobia's words.

"Just so. Valuable but worthless if you can't extract it. The power that comes closest to the energy that makes up what we call magic is human emotion. The power in one person is negligible, but a large group of people can generate an almost limitless amount of energy."

"Emotion? You mean like love?"

"Powerful, I agree," conceded Feldspar, "but impossible to generate artificially. Avarice, on the other hand, is far simpler to create. All we needed to do was gather a lot of humans and the tantalizing possibility of something for nothing."

"The claims," I whispered. "The Dragonlands."

"Precisely. At eleven fifty-nine and fifty-five seconds, there were eight million people staring anxiously at their watches, their hearts beating faster, the sweat rising on their brows in expectation of claiming enough land to retire. Greed is all powerful; greed conquers all. Greed channeled the Big Magic; greed set us free."

"But why leave so much to chance?"

"Big Magic works in mysterious ways, Jennifer. If you push destiny, it has a nasty habit of pushing back. All things must come together in confluence. There had to be you, Dragondeath by Exhorbitus, and all that raw emotion. Once Maltcassion was sure you were ready, he used the last of the dragon magic to send out the premonition of his own death and a broad feeling of greed that caught on like a virus. He knew a bit about ConStuff and a lot about human nature. Once the crowds were gathered, the death of a dragon would kick-start the spell, you as the Berzerker would draw the power from those around you, and Exhorbitus would channel the power. I think you'll agree that it all turned out rather well."

I digested what Feldspar had said. Maltcassion had sown, farmed, and then harvested the emotional energy from eight million people. The dragons had defeated the most powerful wizard the world had ever known, and taken over four hundred years to do it. Maltcassion had given his life to make it happen. I sighed.

"We sense your sorrow, Jennifer. If it's any consolation, there is much in us that was Maltcassion. He hasn't gone for good; he just, well, *fragmented* slightly."

"So what happens now?"

"Well," said Colin. "The Dragonslayer's work is done. We will live here and grow strong. We want peace with humans and have much to teach you. You will come and see us, and you will be our ambassador. We thank you again for all you have done."

I picked up Exhorbitus from where it had fallen. It was a fine weapon, worthy of a Berzerker if he or she were to ever have need of it. When I grew older and was stronger, perhaps I might even learn to wield it with skill. I bowed to both dragons using the traditional method of departure, and they returned the wishes. I walked a few paces, then turned back. There was still one question I wanted to ask.

"Maltcassion used a word just before he died. He called me *Gwanjii*."

"Ah," replied Feldspar solemnly, "that is an old dragon word. A word that one dragon might use to another perhaps twice in his lifetime."

"What does it mean?"

"Friend."

THIRTY-THREE

The End of the Story

I drove back to the marker stones to find that the avaricious spell had broken. Everyone was packing up to leave, wondering why they had sat on a hillside for five days drinking stewed tea and eating stale cake. The landships and artillery stood silent, the soldiers waiting for orders that never came. The Berzerkers had stopped hitting each other with bricks and were calming themselves by doing tricks with yo-yos.

Wizard Moobin met me as I stepped across the boundary. "You did it!" he shouted as he hugged me wildly.

"At a price, Moobin, at a price."

He guessed my meaning and wrapped a blanket

around my shoulders. I was shaking badly and had a fever. My throat was badly inflamed; I would sleep for almost three days.

Within a week, a sea of trash and acres of mud around the Dragonlands was the only evidence that eight million people had waited eagerly for an event that never took place. King Snodd and Brecon did not go to war — or at least, not then. Magic returned to the planet with added vigor. Every one of the sorcerers at Zambini Towers found that their powers had increased; in future, it would be much easier to hire out their talents.

After some legal wranglings and a week in prison, I was granted a reluctant pardon by the king and returned to run Kazam Mystical Arts Management. I keep the sword Exhorbitus in a cupboard in case I have any need for it in the future. Transient Moose is still hanging around Zambini Towers, the Mysterious X has become *more* mysterious, Perkins is almost ready to take his magic test, and Lady Mawgon remains our most aggressive critic. The Great Zambini has still not reappeared, and luckily, neither has the Mighty Shandar — but we hold frequent strategy meetings about what to do if he does.

I was delighted to speak at Mother Zenobia's 182nd birthday party two months later, although we told her it was only her 160th to keep her from getting depressed. I gave the entire Dragonslayer merchandising rights to the

Troll War Widows Association, who made very good use of it. The Consolidated Useful Stuff Land Development Corporation was bankrupt a month later.

We often see the dragons flying over the town as they explore the kingdoms. I give as much time and energy to the Berzerkers' Benevolent Fund as I can, but I never tell anyone why. I am careful never to lose my temper. It's safer that way.

As for the Quarkbeast, without whom there would be no Jennifer Strange and thus no Big Magic or dragons, we thought it would be fitting to raise a large statue in his honor outside Zambini Towers. Several people screamed and fainted at the unveiling, and the statue often frightens animals and small children.

I think it's what he would have wanted.

Turn the page for a sneak pe– at
book 2 of The Chronicles of Kazam,
The Song of the Quarkbeast!

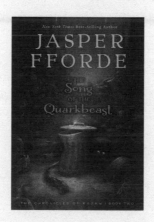

The Rolls-Royce was a top-of-the-line six-wheeled Phantom Twelve. It was as big as a yacht and twice as luxurious, and it had paint work so perfect, the vehicle looked like a pool of black paint sitting in the air. The chauffeur opened the rear passenger door, and a well-dressed girl climbed out. She was not much older than I was, but she came from a world of privilege, cash, and entitlement. I should have hated her, but I didn't.

I envied her.

"Miss Strange?" she said, striding confidently forward, hand outstretched. "Miss Shard is glad to make your acquaintance."

"Who's she talking about?" asked Tiger under his breath, looking around.

"Herself, I think." I smiled broadly to welcome her. "Good morning, Miss Shard. Thank you for coming. I'm Jennifer Strange."

This was our client. She didn't look old enough to have lost something important enough to call us, but you never knew.

"One must call me Ann," she said kindly. "Your recent exploits of a magical variety filled one with a sense of thrilling trepidation."

She was talking in Longspeak, the formal language of the upper classes, and it seemed that she was not fluent in Shortspeak, the everyday language of the Ununited Kingdoms.

"I'm sorry?"

"It was a singular display of inspired audaciousness," she replied.

"Is that good?" I asked, still unsure of her meaning.

"Most certainly," she replied. "We followed your adventures with great interest."

"We?"

"Myself and my client. A gentleman of some consequence, sagacity, and countenance."

She was undoubtedly referring to someone of nobility. Royals in the Ununited Kingdoms employed others to do almost everything for them; only the very poorest nobles did anything for themselves. It was said that when King Wozzle of Snowdonia tired of eating, he employed someone to do it for him. After the inevitable weight loss and death, he was succeeded by his brother.

"I can't understand a word she's saying," whispered Tiger.

"Tiger," I said, keen to get rid of him before she took offense, "why not fetch Full Price and Lady Mawgon, hmm?"

"Were they of a disingenuous countenance?" Miss Shard asked, smiling politely.

"Were who of what?"

"The dragons," she said. "Were they . . . unpleasant?"

"Not really," I replied, guarded. I had some history with dragons, and almost everyone wanted to know about them. I revealed little; dragons value discretion more than anything. I said nothing more, and she got the message.

"I defer to your circumspection on this issue," she replied with a slight bow.

"O . . . kay," I said, not really getting that, either. "This is the team."

Tiger had returned with Full Price and Lady Mawgon, followed by Perkins in his observing capacity. I introduced them all, and Miss Shard said something about how it was "entirely convivial" and "felicitous" to meet them on "this auspicious occasion," and in return they shook hands but remained wary. It pays to distance oneself from clients, especially ones who use too many long words.

"What do you want us to find?" asked Lady Mawgon, who always got straight to the point.

"It's a ring that belonged to the mother of my client," the girl said. "He would be here personally to present his request but finds himself unavailable due to a prolonged sabbatical."

"Has he seen a doctor about it?" asked Tiger.

"About what?"

"His prolonged sabbatical. It sounds very painful."

She stared at him for a moment. "It means he's on vacation."

"Oh."

"I apologize for the ignorance of the staff," said Lady Mawgon, glaring at Tiger, "but Kazam sadly requires foundling labor to function. Staff can be so difficult these days, wanting frivolous little luxuries like food, shoes, wages . . . and human dignity."

"Please don't worry," said Miss Shard politely. "Foundlings can be refreshingly direct sometimes."

"About the ring?" I asked, uncomfortable with all this talk of foundlings.

"Nothing remarkable," replied Miss Shard. "Gold, plain, large like a thumb ring. My client is eager to present it to his mother as a seventieth birthday gift."

"Not a problem," remarked Full Price. "Do you have anything that might have been in contact with this ring?"

"Such as your client's mother?" said Tiger in an impish manner.

"There's this," replied Miss Shard, producing a ring from her pocket. "This was on her middle finger, and rubbed against the lost ring. You can observe the marks. Look."

Lady Mawgon took the ring and stared at it intently for a moment before she clenched it in her fist, murmured something, and then opened her hand. The ring hovered an inch above her open palm, revolving slowly. She passed it to Full Price, who held it up to the light and then popped it into his mouth, clicked it against his fillings for a moment, and then swallowed it.

"Meant to do that," he said in the tone of someone who didn't.

"Really?" asked Miss Shard dubiously, surely wondering how she was going to get it back and in what condition.

"Don't worry," said Price cheerfully. "Amazing how powerful cleaning agents are these days."

"Why did you ask us to meet you here?" asked Lady Mawgon.

It was a good question. We were at an unremarkable rest area on the Ross-Hereford Road near a village called Harewood End.

"This is where she lost it," replied Miss Shard. "It was in her possession when she egressed from her vehicle, and when she departed she didn't have it anymore."

Lady Mawgon looked at me, then at our client, then at Full Price. She smelled the air, mumbled something, and looked thoughtful for a moment.

"This ring is still around here somewhere," she said, "and it's been lost for thirty-two years, ten months, and nine days. Am I correct?"

Miss Shard stared at her. It appeared this was indeed true, and it was impressive. Mawgon had picked up the lingering memory that human emotion can instill on even the most inert of objects.

"Something that stays lost that long is lost for a good reason," added Full Price. "Why doesn't your client give his mother some chocolates instead?"

"Or flowers," said Lady Mawgon. "We can't help you. Good day." She turned to move away.

"We'll pay you a thousand moolah."

Lady Mawgon stopped. A thousand moolah was serious cash.

"A thousand?"

"My client is inclined toward generosity regarding his mother."

Lady Mawgon looked at Full Price, then at me.

"Five thousand," she said.

"Five thousand?" echoed Ann Shard. "To find a ring?"

"This ring *shouldn't* be found," replied Lady Mawgon. "The price reflects the risks."

Miss Shard looked at us all in turn.

"I accept," she said at last, "and I will wait here for results. But no find, no fee. Not even a call-out charge."

"We usually charge for an attempt—" I began, but Mawgon cut me short.

"We're agreed," she said, and made a grimace that might have been her version of a smile.